CROOKED MAN

Also by Tony Dunbar

Delta Time

Against the Grain

Hard Traveling
(with Linda Kravitz)

Our Land Too

CROOKED MAN

Tony Dunbar

G. P. PUTNAM'S SONS
NEW YORK

This book is fiction. All of the characters and settings are purely imaginary. There is no Tubby Dubonnet or Sheriff Mulé, and the real New Orleans is different from their make-believe city.

G. P. Putnam's Sons
Publishers Since 1838
200 Madison Avenue
New York, NY 10016

Library of Congress Cataloging-in-Publication Data

Dunbar, Anthony P.
Crooked man / Tony Dunbar.
p.   cm.
ISBN 0-399-13973-7
1. Lawyers—Louisiana—New Orleans—Fiction.
2. New Orleans (La.)—Fiction.   I. Title.
PS3554.U46336C76   1994   94-5072 CIP
813'.54—dc20

Designed by Rhea Braunstein

Printed in the United States of America
2   3   4   5   6   7   8   9   10

ACKNOWLEDGMENTS

My thanks to Anne Francis, Randall E. Greene, M. Charles Wallfisch, John Sinclair, Jack Alltmont, Will D. Campbell, Bunny Matthews, Janie Baum, John Egerton, and especially to my sister, Linda Kravitz, my agent, Kristin Lindstrom, and murder-novel consultant Trish Still, for reading this book in its formative stages and always saying the right things.

To Kyle Alexander,
the special man

PREFACE

THE PAIN THAT SAID HE WAS drinking too much started creeping up behind Tubby's ears. Raisin Partlow, his drinking buddy, had given up trying to make conversation with him and was puffing on a cigarette in the exaggerated way that irregular smokers do. The dusty, barely lit tavern was thinning out, leaving just a few whiskered pool players chalking up a last game and a pair of busty girls sharing confidences with the even heftier dame behind the bar.

"Never screw a client and never lie to the judge," Tubby said abruptly.

It took Raisin a second to break through to the surface.

"What's that?" he asked.

"That's all of the so-called legal ethics that make sense to me. The rest of it is just so many little rules you can twist around to suit whatever you want to do."

"Well, you know, Tubby, I lied to a judge just last week." Raisin expelled a wobbly smoke ring and smiled in satisfaction. "Old 'Fuzzy' Baer appointed me to represent the fool who shot a fourteen-year-old girl, after he raped her and her mother. He asks me, 'Mr. Partlow, can you put aside your personal feelings and represent this man to the best of your goddamn abilities?'"

The bartender broke off her conversation to look in their direction. Tubby raised his fingers an inch off the scarred oak surface, so cool to the touch, and shook his head, no. The familiar pain of too much whiskey and too much sweet Coca-Cola had already spread over to the top of his skull.

"What did you tell him?"

"I told him, 'Yes, Your Honor. The man deserves his day in court.' I should have told him, 'Fuck no, Judge. I hate this guy. Take him away where I don't have to look at him. Christ, sir, I'll be embarrassed to admit to my godchildren that I was even in the same room with the guy.' But I knew that was the wrong answer to the question."

"You should have told him the truth," Tubby said.

"Like what?"

"You should have said, 'Heck no, Judge. But I'll do a better job than anybody else you're likely to get."

Raisin shrugged and waved at the bartender. Tubby slid off his stool and grabbed the bar for support.

"I'm out of here," he said.

Raisin looked concerned about being left alone.

"Let me buy you one more," he said. "The night is still young."

"No, I'm good. Tomorrow is a school day." Tubby let go of the bar to test his footing. So far, so good. He laid two dollar bills on his wet napkin and waved goodbye to the barmaid. He patted Raisin on the back and suddenly found himself on the sidewalk outside. A DIXIE BEER sign blinked and crickets sang in the weeds sprouting from the curb. All the houses were closed up tight, and the only people around were a couple of shadowy heads in a parked car down the street. Tubby located his own car, but had a hard time getting the key into the door lock. His head was pounding and he bent over to rest it on the smooth metal roof, misted with dew, until the night air restored his vision.

He conceded to himself that he had lost another round in his ongoing battle with the great drug alcohol, but he decided not to let this be his final encounter. Jamming his keys back into his pants pocket, Tubby began an unsteady march away from the river and in the general direction of home. Dogs barked through curtained windows at him, and stray cats peered around the tires of parked cars to watch his progress.

What was it, maybe thirty-five blocks? Just a couple of miles. Maybe he would be sobered up by the time he got there. Maybe he'd try jogging it. Better save his energy in case he needed to run for real. He picked up the pace anyway, and his course straightened—a solitary lawyer bobbing along through dark neighborhoods, navigating by the moon.

ONE

"MAN, IT'S HARD TO GET UP for work when it's raining like this." Freddie took a bite out of his bacon, egg, and cheese biscuit and stared morosely at the rain coming down in sheets outside the McDonald's on Carrollton Avenue.

"As little work as you do, Freddie, I wouldn't complain," the big man sitting across the plastic table said. He had broad, square shoulders, and his fingers wrapped entirely around the cup of coffee he was holding.

"What job did you ever put me on that I didn't do? I'm asking you." Freddie looked offended.

"Sure, you do everything right, but I have to keep my eyes on you the whole time."

"That ain't fair, Casey."

Casey took a sip of coffee. He watched some telephone company workers run from their truck into the restaurant. They were slinging rainwater off their sleeves when they passed, and a couple of drops caught Casey on the cheek.

"Christ!" he protested, but the men paid no attention to him. He contemplated Freddie, who was pushing the last of the biscuit into his mouth.

"Okay. Here's a job for you, Freddie. We're going to take some money away from a drug runner."

Freddie gulped down what he was chewing. "Huh?" he said. He poked a finger in his mouth to search.

"That's a bad habit you have, making me repeat everything. It's an important job I'm talking about. We can see what you're capable of doing."

"What do you mean, drugs? Wouldn't it, you know, look bad for us to be doing drug stuff?"

"Listen up, Freddie." Casey leaned across the table to get closer to Freddie's face. "I don't give a shit about drugs. We're just going to take the criminals' money. We're the good guys."

"Oh," Freddie nodded. "How much money?" he asked.

"You'll get enough. I'll take care of you."

"What's my job?"

"Backup. Enforcement. Whatever the fuck I tell you to do."

"Could somebody get hurt?" Freddie asked, which was a dumb question.

"Oh, yeah," Casey said. "I think it's a distinct possibility there could be some mayhem involved with this. Maybe a little blood on the streets, here and there. You'd be up for that, wouldn't you?"

Freddie thought for a second, but not very deeply.

"Just tell me what to do, boss." He put on a goofy grin

and rolled his eyes back in his head, like a comedian he had seen on TV, trying to get a chuckle out of Casey.

Casey wouldn't give it to him.

"Just finish your fucking McMuffin, Freddie, and let's get out of here."

TWO

UBBY DUBONNET TOYED
with a silver salad fork, heavy as a sugar bowl. "This is the
most complicated appetizer I've ever seen," he told Dr.
Feingold. The arrangement that the black-vested waiter had
just placed in front of him involved three almost-round
crawfish beignets flecked with tiny specks of pimento. They
were accompanied by a second plate decorated with skinny
fettuccine noodles, lettuce leaves, and curled ribbons of
carrots. The waiter was explaining that the chef suggested
taking each beignet, rolling it and the vegetables up in a
lettuce leaf, and dipping it all into a little china bowl of
orange sauce which completed the dish. There were also
mint leaves, but Tubby missed what he was supposed to do
with those.

"It is a little work," Dr. Feingold said when the waiter
departed, "but I think you'll find it very refreshing. Don't
you love what they've done with this place?"

"Very nice," Tubby agreed. The air floated gently from

the ceiling fans rotating lazily over the newly painted dining room with its row of windows along St. Charles Avenue. A casual mix of coat-and-tie office workers and the homeless, civilization's stragglers, looking for shade, a handout, or a little hope, drifted through the heat outside. Now and then traveling teenagers carrying backpacks passed—Europeans, maybe, but since so many kids had started wearing black you couldn't really tell. The diners, cool and tranquil, watched the passersby like fish, observing the world from inside the glass of an aquarium. Every ten minutes or so a streetcar rumbled by.

The old hotel upstairs had struggled for years. It had been kept alive by Governor Edwards and his legion of lawyers who occupied an entire one of its floors for months while the Governor was on trial for bribery. His acquittal had suddenly left the place empty, but, a bankruptcy or two later, it was making a celebrated comeback. Now aproned waiters scattered warm pistolettes of French bread and ro-settes of iced butter before an appreciative flock of feasting gastronomes with heavy-metal credit cards.

Tubby ordered a duo of softshell crabs. Dr. Feingold had the trout. The crabs came with a creamy herb sauce on the side, which Tubby dolloped lavishly onto his plate with only a twinge of guilt. I'm not in such bad shape after forty-five years and roughly half as many Mardi Gras, he told himself. A small paunch, maybe, but I can still go out on a public beach. He still had most of his thick blond hair, and he was vain enough to think that the way it turned golden in the summer sunshine complemented his tan. By nature, Tubby took a charitable view of both himself and others. He had a sportsman's face, blue eyes spaced far apart in a guileless countenance that could not conceal a blush. Suit jackets strained against his broad shoulders and barrel chest, and often people's first impression of him was correct—he was their college football lineman, domesticated and brought into harness. His nails were even and clean, as a lawyer's should be, though his knuckles showed surprising scars. Tubby had not worn jewelry on his hands since he took off his wedding ring.

"How was your trip?" he asked.

"Wonderful," Dr. Feingold said enthusiastically. "Costa Rica is such a beautiful country. We stayed in a fantastic hotel, and nearby there was a crystal clear lagoon, a perfect blue, with superb snorkeling. It was lovely. Have you ever snorkeled, Tubby?"

"Sure, when I was a kid. But I didn't even know grown-ups did it for fun until you started going on about it."

"It's a great sport. You see things you never imagined."

"Actually, Marty, I get enough of that in my law practice. What I see walking around on the streets amazes me on a daily basis. But I know what you mean."

"You ought to give it a try. Live a little. You would enjoy the peace and quiet."

"I'm sure I would. Too bad you have to submerge yourself in the ocean to get some."

"Let's talk about my case," Dr. Feingold said, slipping an ivory bit of fish on his fork. "I really feel bad about Sandy, but don't you think his demands are just a wee bit outrageous?"

"It does look like you botched the operation up, Marty. In all honesty, I feel funny representing him."

"You shouldn't. I'm much more comfortable with you

doing it than one of those ambulance-chasers out there. I trust you to treat me fairly."

"It just seems strange to me that when a guy thinks you've destroyed his epidermis he'd still take your recommendation for a lawyer."

Sandy Shandell was an exotic. The first time he had come into Tubby's office, Cherrylynn, Tubby's secretary, had shown him to a chair and then breathlessly rushed in to tell her boss, shutting the door behind her so that Sandy wouldn't hear, "Mr. Dubonnet. There is a man outside to see you, and he's wearing makeup."

"He's an entertainer. They all wear stuff on their faces."

"I'd sure like to see the entertainment he puts on. He's wearing the same eye shadow as me," she giggled and blushed.

"Calm down, Cherrylynn. Just show him in."

She did, but as she stood behind Sandy, a tall sinewy man who did indeed paint his face, she made hand signals and, eyes big as pies, silently mouthed, "Do you see?"

"Hold my calls," Tubby said and closed the door on her.

The next time Sandy came for an office visit he presented Cherrylynn with a tiny cloisonné pin.

"I just thought it would match your hair," he said, and she was completely won over. After that when he called or came by the office, he and Cherrylynn would chat like sisters until Tubby would break them up so he could get some work done.

"Sure it sounds funny for a patient to ask his doctor to suggest a malpractice lawyer," Dr. Feingold continued, "but Sandy has this unshakable conviction, formed years ago when I adjusted his nose, that I'm the most intelligent person he knows. He still relies on me, even if the skin-darkening treatments were less than totally successful."

"He should have been satisfied with the way he was," Tubby said philosophically as he tried with little success to spear a pod of snowpeas.

"If everybody felt that way, Tubby, plastic surgeons would be out of a job. We exist because it is a human instinct to want to change. We aspire. Sandy's hero, for example, is a television show cop, some guy—I can't think of his name—with a real Caribbean, coffee-and-cream look. But Sandy's natural pigment is paler than mine. He didn't just want to look tan, mind you. I could have handled that easy. He wanted to look like a Creole gambler. Those were his words to me. That enchanting picture inspired me, and it's what got me into this mess."

"He's kind of splotchy now," Tubby observed.

"I told him the treatments were experimental," Dr. Feingold said defensively. "I told him there was very little literature in the area. I told him there was a chance this could happen. God knows, I feel sorry about it."

Tubby patted his lips with his napkin. "Look out, Marty. Sandy has got a good case. My first job is to do right by him. You and I have been friends for a long time, but I've got to represent Sandy to the best of my ability, just like I do every other client."

"I understand that, and I wouldn't expect anything less, knowing you as I do. But surely Sandy Shandell does not have a three-million-dollar case."

Marty Feingold had sad puppy eyes below bushy eyebrows, and Tubby felt them probing his, looking for pity.

"Who knows. More than a hundred grand, probably.

Juries are unpredictable. If Sandy can keep it together on the stand, those twelve noble citizens in the jury box could do you some real damage."

"My insurance rates will skyrocket." Now it looked like the doctor was close to tears. He was even forgetting to eat.

"It's just the price of doing business," Tubby consoled him. "You'll just raise your fees, right?"

The thought seemed to comfort Dr. Feingold. He picked up an almond slice with his fingers and nibbled it. "I suppose that's true," he said.

Tubby pressed ahead. "There will always be tummies to tuck," he said. A waiter passing with a fudge-drenched piece of chocolate cake caught his attention. "Hey, would you look at that dessert."

"Help yourself."

"No, I've got too much work to do this afternoon. I think that would put me out of commission for at least a couple of hours."

"Then I'll get the check."

"No. This one is on me, Marty. You sent me a good client."

"I have this feeling I'm going to end up paying for it."

"I can't argue with that."

"Hmmm."

Tubby and Marty Feingold strolled together across Lafayette Square in the direction of Tubby's office and Marty's car. A crew of gardeners, mostly Asian women wearing pointed hats, squatted around a fountain, pulling weeds from a bed of vividly colored pansies. A family of pigeons, like toy soldiers, waddled over to them hopefully then fluttered excitedly out of the way.

"They're doing a great job keeping the place up," Dr. Feingold said, nodding at the industrious laborers and the neatly trimmed border around the concrete fountain.

"Yes, they are. Most of them don't speak any English, you know. It's hard to imagine going to a strange country halfway around the world and ending up tending flowers in the parks of a city where you don't even speak the language. They sure can understand the flowers, though, can't they?"

"In ten years they'll own this town."

"Everybody else has taken a turn at running New Orleans, why not them?"

"They couldn't do much worse than we've done, could they?"

"Wake up, Marty. We're not in charge here anymore."

"We're just allowed to show up for work, right?"

"Work and play," said Tubby. "And that's not too shabby."

They shook hands and parted underneath the Whitney Bank clock on the streetcorner. A delivery kid, riding a bicycle the wrong way down the street, almost collided with Dr. Feingold in the crosswalk.

"Sorry," the kid shouted, laughing, and kept on pedaling, a carefree two-wheeled traveler through a land of overheated cars stuck waiting for the light and burning plenty of gas.

One of the gardeners straightened up to wipe the sweat from her forehead with the loose sleeve of her jacket. She looked at the line of cars, and in a red one not far away she saw a man that she knew. Quickly, she put her head down and buried her hands deeply in the soft dirt.

Casey pressed the horn down and held it.

"What's the problem?" he yelled out the window to nobody in particular.

Freddie leaned out his side to look.

"I think they're letting cars out of the garage. I don't see no accident."

"What do women expect you to think when they go around exposed like that?" Casey muttered, looking over a pair of sharply dressed secretaries strolling along the sidewalk on their lunch break. He spied the gardener and chuckled when she ducked.

"It's indecent," Freddie agreed.

"You see that skinny gook over there? The one squatting by that bush?"

"Yeah, sure."

"They call her Panda. Her brother got locked up, breaking and entering, car theft, something like that. Her family makes the right connections, and it comes around to me that they want him treated okay in jail. You know, where nobody bothers him, and he gets to have his cigarettes and his little personal items without any hassle. No big thing. I'm dealing with Bin Minny on this, you know who I mean?"

"I seen him around. I think I seen him talking to you."

"Yeah, well, he's the king gook out in New Orleans East, where they all live. You know, you don't see no dogs running loose out there."

Freddie laughed.

Casey gunned the motor, keeping an eye on the temperature gauge. The traffic seemed permanently stalled.

"This little girl, Panda, comes to see me at the office,"
Casey continued. By "office" Freddie understood him to
mean BB Bail Bonds—across from the Criminal Courts
building, where Casey had a desk and phone and generally
hung out most of the time—not Casey's official office at the
jail. He rarely went there, but he allowed Freddie to use it
if he needed a private place to take a nap or eat a pizza that
he didn't want to share.

"I don't know how she knew who I was, but she comes
in, 'Missa Casey,' she says. She can hardly talk English. But
she tells me that Bin Minny is raising the price for looking
after her brother and she can't pay it. So he offers to let her
work it out as one of his girls, and she can make lots of
money that way. She don't like that, so she comes to see
me."

"What'd you tell her?" Freddie asked.

"I told her to get the hell out of my office. Like I'm gonna
mess up my friendly relations with Bin Minny 'cause this
little girl, who has an asshole for a brother, can't get along.
She leaves like she don't understand how 'Big Missa Sheriff
Casey' can say that, but she gets the message. Right away
I call Bin Minny to tell him one of his people is off the
reservation and, real cool, he asks me, as a favor, to wise up
the brother. I pass the word, and two of the guys at the jail
work the brother over a little bit. That was right before you
got here, Freddie. If you'd been on my team then, it would
have been a good job for you."

"I wouldn't have minded," Freddie said.

"And what do you know, the next week the payments

are being made again, the brother gets over his scrapes and bruises, and Bin Minny owes me a favor. My only regret is I probably should have poked her while I had the chance, but I don't like gooks."

"It's all pink on the inside," Freddie offered.

"That's a very humorous observation, Freddie," Casey said. "Speaking of which, I just remembered we're supposed to pass by the Starburst Lounge today and pick up our present."

"I could do that this afternoon, if you're busy," Freddie suggested.

"You'd like to go by yourself, wouldn't you, Freddie? That way you collect a little extra, right?"

"No, nothing like that, Casey. I was just saying I'd go. Then I'd bring it over to your office—if you got something else to do."

"I appreciate your volunteer spirit. Some initiative is a good thing. But not too much."

Sitting around in traffic was putting Casey in a dangerous mood, and Freddie wanted to change the subject.

"When are we going to do that job you were talking about—with the drug runner?" he asked.

"It isn't something you need to worry about yet. The money is out there as we speak. I haven't quite got a fix on it yet, but I will. Then I'll let you know it's time to answer the bell."

"I'll be ready, whenever."

"Let's move it," Casey shouted out the window. The block-long line of cars didn't budge.

"Let's try out the light and see if we can get through this," Casey said.

Freddie put the blue flasher on top of the dashboard and flipped the switch. Casey blew the horn, bounced two wheels up on the curb, and started squeezing through. This was one of the times he wished he was a city cop. He would love to have a loudspeaker he could use to make these fools get out of the way. Only thing, there wasn't any money in being a cop.

THREE

PEOPLE OFTEN ASKED TUBBY what his day was like—how it was being a lawyer in a city like New Orleans. He knew there was no way to describe it, all the sad and comic touches. He just knew he wasn't often bored.

He parked his red Thunderbird convertible by the abandoned, boarded-up Falstaff brewery off Broad Street and scrambled across four busy lanes to the plaza in front of Traffic Court. Inside the masses were gathering for afternoon services, reduced to the common denominator of having to explain away yellow lights that turned red, school-zone signs hidden behind crepe myrtle trees, and Breathalyzer machines that gave out faulty readings.

Courtroom C was filled with at least a hundred people, each waiting for his name to be called by the clerk up front, a balding man with a lumpy nose and a wrinkled tie named Moses Seamster, who had mastered an attitude of total indifference to everything. His foghorn voice summoned a few more offenders every few minutes to come forward and plead with him about their cases. He disposed of the vast majority in ten seconds and fewer words, accepting their plea, fixing their fine, and sending them off to pay. The judge was nowhere to be seen. A handful of bored-looking lawyers hung out on the front row and around a door leading to the back room where an assistant city attorney considered more grievous offenses and dealt with citizens who refused to plead guilty. Tubby was acquainted with a bunch of the regulars, and he walked up to join them.

"Hiya Walter, whatcha got today?" he asked an older attorney he knew, a tall gentleman wearing a shiny gray suit and holding his briefcase across his narrow chest like it might stop a bullet.

"Hey, Tubby. DWI. Drove into the bushes off Wisner into City Park. My issue is no one saw him actually driving the vehicle, and he wasn't on a public thoroughfare when the cops pulled him out of the shrubbery. So where's the crime? It's bullshit, maybe, but we'll see. What's yours?"

"My client is Monster Mudbug," Tubby said.

"What, the guy you see at Mardi Gras?"

"That's him. Oh no, here he is."

Monster Mudbug drove a tow truck by trade. He had spotted Tubby and was walking up the aisle dressed in dusty blue jeans, a spray-painted surfer shirt, and blue sunglasses. He paused at the swinging wooden gate and waved, and Tubby went over to collect him.

"Jesus, I told you to clean up, Adrian."

"Couldn't, Mr. Tubby. I was working."

"You must have been working under a car."

"Yeah, there was a three-car wreck up on the high rise. Two other guys beat me there, so I had to scoop the worst car, which had both its front tires completely mangled. First I had to wait for the ambulance and the rescue guys to get the people out."

"Were they hurt?"

"Yeah, pretty bad. The guy was some kind of preacher, and these leaflets about a revival or something were blowing out of his car and all over the highway. This pretty lady that was in the car with him got banged on the head. She was walking around in circles saying, 'Reverend James, Reverend James.' " Adrian tried to imitate her. "She had blood just dripping off her."

Tubby shook his head in sympathy. "Listen, Adrian . . ." he began.

"Yeah, I was kind of worried that the old man might be dead. The ambulance driver said he'd pull through, though. But I guess if he'd of died he would have gone straight to heaven. Don't you think? Baptists believe in heaven, don't they?"

"Sure they do, Adrian. Did you think it was just a Catholic thing? But now that you're here, did you bring proof of insurance?"

"Yeah, sixty days."

"I don't know if they'll take that. You need real insurance."

"It's hard to get insurance on the Rolling Boiler," Adrian lamented. He was speaking about a chopped-down Ford Escort chassis he had decorated with papier-mâché and sheet metal to look like a huge crawfish pot. He had girls, pretty ones if he could get them, dress up like crawfish and jump around in the pot. He used it for parties and parades and was trying to get recognized as a local character.

"I'll bet the Moss Man doesn't have insurance," he complained.

"I know the Moss Man, and he does have insurance," Tubby told him. "Plus he has a brake tag, too."

"I'd like to know where he gets it. They'd just laugh at me if I pulled into a brake tag station. Can you imagine?"

"Give me your certificate of insurance and I'll see what I can do."

Adrian sat on the bench while Tubby squeezed through the crowd to the hallway behind the courtroom where whatever assistant city attorney had the duty that day met with lawyers and regular folks to conduct the real business of the court, which was to hammer out guilty pleas. Today he found Risi Shexnayder, a young lawyer he had seen before over at the law school, sitting behind a little desk, interrogating a fat black teenager while a policeman, lounging on a folding chair in the corner, picked his teeth with a wooden match.

The teenager was telling a story about why he ran a stop sign. The cop interrupted to say he didn't believe the kid then and he didn't believe him now, and, in any case, running a stop sign was against the law, so why not cut the crap. The kid finally agreed to pay a fine, but he was mad about it. He collected his papers and strutted out.

Shexnayder waved Tubby toward the empty chair. She was in her twenties but was already getting the worn-and-tired appearance that comes from spending too much time cooped up in windowless rooms with petty offenders and cops.

"Hey, Mr. Dubonnet, where y'at? I know it must be a major bust for a big shot like you to be down here."

"No, this is not a big deal, Risi. Today I represent Monster Mudbug. Grabbed for no insurance, tag, or title on his way to the Saint Patrick's Day Parade in the Irish Channel."

"Yeah. I saw him in that parade. He wears this big chef's hat and was throwing boiled crawfish and potatoes, right? That's a crazy guy. Is that stuff legal? It must be a health-code violation. So what do you want me to do?"

"Forget the whole thing. No one gets title or tags on something like that. I mean, it's a float, really. And anyway he's got insurance."

The assistant city attorney inspected the insurance certificate Tubby pushed across her desk.

"This is from Blue Streak Insurance Company," she said. "They've been out of business for months. This is no good."

Tubby looked at it again. "So, you're right. But that's not the kid's fault. See, he paid the premium."

"I hope he can get his money back. Judge is hard on no insurance, but I guess maybe this counts for something. Monster Mudbug has to have a license tag, though. If it runs on gas and rolls down the street you gotta put a tag on it. We'll throw everything else out if he pays a hundred and twenty-five dollars plus costs."

"Okay," Tubby said. The prosecutor scribbled some notes on the tickets and handed them to Tubby.

"Take these to the clerk, and it's all taken care of. And

say hello to Reggie Turntide for me." Reggie was Tubby's partner.

"You know Reggie?" Tubby was surprised because Reggie had probably never ventured into Traffic Court.

"I met him at the fish fry my boss, the City Attorney, has every summer for all of us and the politicians. Reggie was really sweet. He played with my little boy for about two hours."

"Yeah, Reggie really likes kids."

"He seemed to. You can tell Monster Mudbug I think his whole, uh, presentation is outasight. People go crazy trying to catch those crawfish. They had a good flavor, too."

"You ate them?"

"Sure, I wasn't thinking too clearly at the time."

"I'll tell him he has an admirer in Traffic Court." Tubby grabbed the tickets and was out the door. The next lawyer in line stepped forward quickly and sat on the chair. One more man with a story to tell.

Adrian had found some friends in the courtroom, and they were all talking to each other in whispers, out of respect for where they were, but there was still no judge in sight.

"I got her to throw out the no title, no brake tag, and no insurance," Tubby told him, "but you'll have to pay a hundred and twenty-five dollars plus costs for no license tag." Adrian's friends were impressed.

"That's good," Adrian said. "I brought two hundred dollars with me just in case."

"What you do is pay your lawyer first. Give me the two hundred dollars."

"What do I pay the fine with?"

"They'll give you time. Go to the back and work it out

with the lady. Pay me the two hundred dollars. And get some real insurance. The city attorney back there likes you. She caught your show and loved it, but there's a price for fame. You can't let down all the people who are getting behind you. Monster Mudbug is the kind of guy who has insurance."

"I see that, Mr. Tubby. I can't be getting into legal hassles all the time. I gotta think about my fans. There's a lot of young people who look up to me."

"Right, Adrian. You gotta be an example to them."

"Sure. Thanks for everything, Mr. Tubby." They said goodbye and parted ways.

How did I ever get into this line of work, Tubby asked himself as he pushed open the glass doors to the world outside. He gave a couple of bucks to the young lad who was watching his car and got a barely perceptible nod in return. He wasn't sure, but it looked to Tubby as though his wheel covers had been shined.

FOUR

MONIQUE WAS A SMALL-
town girl. She had come to what to her was the big city of
New Orleans from Evergreen, Alabama, home of a million
slash pine trees and a Holiday Inn. She was running away
from home at age twenty-three.

The immediate goal was to get away from Ned, her ex-
husband, who liked to punch her about once a week while
they were married and periodically came around for similar
recreation after they got divorced. She got started on her
escape after he almost ran her off the Interstate one night
with his four-by-four pickup truck, pushing her onto the
shoulder, saved only by an exit ramp which appeared just
in time. She swerved up it and took refuge under the dusty
vapor lamps of an all-night convenience store, leaving Ned
to clip the signpost and navigate his drunken way north.
Then she shook and shook, waiting for her mother to get
her landlord to come and escort her home. She stared at the
pretty faces beckoning from the shiny magazine covers on

the rack by the phone and decided that her only hope for a real life lay in flight.

As soon as she was convoyed back to her trailer she dragged out her most precious belongings and threw them into her dented, still-not-paid-for Rabbit. She dropped the keys to her mobile home in the manager's mailbox, drove out to Interstate 65 and turned south, for no reason but that Ned lived five miles to the north in Owassa and she was taking no chances on running into him again that night. A long two hours later, when only eighteen-wheelers and other lonely pilgrims were on the highway, a slender corridor through dark miles of uninhabited and forbidding pine forests, she stopped for gas and cigarettes in Mobile. Mixed in with the truck fumes she could smell the salt in the air. The road east went to Pensacola, where she and Ned had once taken a beach trip during their brief courtship. The sign to the west said New Orleans. She had never been there. It sounded a lot better than anyplace she had ever gone with Ned. If she didn't find something there, like safety, a place to work, or romance, then she could just keep going to Texas, or maybe even California.

"How many hours is it to New Orleans?" she asked the sleepy-looking man behind the counter.

"About three, if you don't stop," he said. "Are you planning on going all the way through tonight?"

"Yep." She made up her mind.

"You reckon that car of yours will make it that far?" he asked.

"It had better," she said, pocketing her change.

"I'm just pointing out, ladies have to be careful at night.

There ain't nothing much out there but dark for the next a hundred and forty miles."

"Thanks, but I'm not worried," she said. And the surprising thing was that she really wasn't worried. "Couldn't I walk a hundred and forty miles?" she asked herself as she settled back behind the wheel.

Coming over a high-rise bridge into the city at daybreak took her breath away. The tall buildings, rising up in the new sun, the graceful outline of the suspension bridges over the Mississippi River, the brawling morning traffic, made a promise to her—a promise of possibilities. She opened the window to let in the cool, clean Gulf of Mexico air, exited at Franklin Avenue, and fell asleep parked in a neighborhood of proud oak trees and old brick houses.

She was rousted by a policeman at around ten a.m. He ascertained that she was alive and told her politely that she needed to move along. After they talked a little, he with his blond mustache and bulky blue jacket, she with sleepy eyes and tangled hair, he suggested a rooming house on Canal Street. He gave her directions and waved when she puttered away. She found the place without trouble. It was a lovely old mansion with a big yard, owned by a blue-haired lady who showed Monique to an immaculate room, furnished with a bed, a dresser, a television, a cherry-red throw rug, and a vase of fresh flowers. It cost as much for a week as her trailer in Evergreen had cost for a month. It was her first house in New Orleans, and there were roses in bloom outside her window.

Monique made her way. Right off the bat her car got

towed from a freight-loading zone while she was using a pay phone, and she never went to pick it up. She was afraid that the finance company might have reported it stolen, and she'd get arrested. She learned the bus routes and found a job as an exotic dancer in a foul-smelling club on Decatur Street. Ali, the linebacker-sized barman, made sure the customers didn't touch her unless she allowed them to, and the money was okay. It was basically good exercise, except that the air in the place, from the customers' cigarettes and other noxious emissions, was roughly the flavor of car exhaust.

She moved out of the rooming house and into a cheap apartment in the French Quarter. It was nice being able to explore the Quarter before work, to walk down to the river and watch the freighters with names of countries she had never heard of painted on their bows, to mingle with tourists and sometimes buy a muffeletta, packed with Italian ham and olive salad, and eat it outdoors in Jackson Square. She bought a bike. She did what she needed to do to get by. She made some friends and picked up a little cocaine habit. A job waiting tables in a bacon-and-eggs joint on Chartres Street opened up, and she took it even though it paid less than dancing. When she walked out of the strip joint, she gave Ali her falsies and G-string, and he got a huge laugh out of that.

Monique did not consider herself to be a genius by any means. Sometimes she wondered if God had given her any brains at all. But when she met Darryl Alvarez at a party her boss threw, she was smart enough to know that he was a step up. He was a little short for her taste, and he had kind of a Spanish look that was new to her, but he seemed real sure of himself and he said a lot of interesting things.

They left the party early and went out and had a few drinks in a crowded bar Uptown run by a friend of his. The drinks were on the house, which was impressive, and Darryl left a fat tip for the waitress, which was even more so. He was fun. They stopped off at his apartment right on Lake Pontchartrain, overlooking what he said was the yacht harbor, to snort a little coke together. His apartment wasn't furnished like the ones most of her previous boyfriends lived in. There weren't any Mexican bullfight pictures on the wall, for one thing. It was all very modern and clean and had wall-to-wall carpet. There was a big wooden cabinet that when he opened it revealed a television and a stereo and some carved black statues from Africa of fierce naked men and women, and he had a thick glass coffee table. She checked out the medicine cabinet while she was in the bathroom and found out that Darryl used Mitchum, Colgate, and Drakkar Noir. It was clean in there, too, which was mighty unusual for a man, and she thought he must have a maid.

Darryl pulled the curtains open, and she could see, across the street and the floodwall, all the sailboats berthed in their little slips in the harbor, illuminated by tiny lights strung along the piers. It was very romantic.

"I'll make it a little darker and you can see the view better," he said, and she giggled.

"That's funny?" he asked, switching off a lamp. "What can I fix for you?"

"Oh, a beer, I guess. I don't care."

"Here's a Miller Lite," he said, handing her a pony bottle, "so you can keep your beautiful figure."

"Thank you. What do you do to stay in shape?"

"I chase after love," he said, and he kissed her on the back of her neck. A shiver ran all the way down her. "It's wonderful exercise."

She ended up spending the night.

In the morning he drove her back downtown to her apartment. He was polite enough to wait until she got inside her gate before he drove away, but she was afraid that would be the end of Darryl. No problem, it had been for kicks. But surprise, he called her later in the week and offered her a job waiting tables at Champ's, which turned out to be his restaurant and bar out by the lake.

"I don't know if you're interested," he said.

"Sure, I'd be interested. What nights would I work?"

"Seven nights a week, if you want to. We just had a girl quit. You can do three or four, it's up to you." With Darryl, she would find out, a lot of things would be up to her.

"You want to come in tomorrow night and see how it goes?" he asked.

"Sure, fine," she said.

"Okay. Be here at four o'clock."

"I'll be there." She had to look in the Yellow Pages to find out where the bar was. Then she called RTA to learn how to get there on a bus. You had to go to Canal, then out to the Lake, then take a bus out Robert E. Lee. Wow! That could take two hours. She told her boss she was sorry, but she was quitting, and she dropped her green apron on the counter.

FIVE

T UBBY DROVE DOWNTOWN ON
Tulane Avenue. It was after four-thirty, and the going-
home traffic was beginning to build up in the opposite
direction. He thought about Tulane Avenue when he first
saw it as a kid, brought to town by his dad for a Pelicans
baseball game. It was really something back then. There
were palm trees on the neutral ground and even a streetcar
line. You ate hot dogs at the stadium, maybe skipped a few
rocks in the New Basin Canal where all the Irishmen had
died of malaria, then watched dad drink a beer at the Home
Plate Inn after the game. Now it was an eight-lane strip for
commuters who rolled past a string of cheap motels and
pimply street whores and kept their windows up.

The baseball stadium was now a hotel that had changed
its name so many times nobody could remember what it
was. There was no place to park on the curbs. You couldn't
make a left turn for a mile. Once you got on the damn street

there was no place to go but downtown. He couldn't imagine how the Chinese groceries on each corner survived. Thinking about these things he pulled up to a light and was beeped at from alongside so loudly that he almost jumped the curb. When he swung around to start swearing he saw it was Jynx Margolis, a client of his who was widely admired for her great sense of style and impressive cleavage.

She lowered her window, letting out a perfumed puff of air so cool that Tubby, in his convertible, could feel the draft six feet away.

"I have to talk to you, Mr. Dubonnet."

That was promising. Apparently she had been doing something athletic. Her white sports shirt with a tiny penguin on it was open at the collar, and she looked like the dessert he had missed at lunch.

"You've got to help me get an injunction or something on Byron. Now the creep is calling me at all hours of the night," she yelled.

"Get call blocking," Tubby shouted.

"No, really, I have to talk to you."

"Come to my office. But it's going to have to be brief." Up went her window, and she zoomed ahead.

Tubby parked at Place Palais. It took just a minute to get to his spot. He had clocked it more than once and found it took about five seconds to navigate every floor when the garage was empty and an incredibly slow minute and a half per floor at rush hour. It gave you a chance to think— usually about places without car fumes. He parked on Level 9 and rode up in the elevator to the forty-third floor of the office building. He went through the door with TURNTIDE & DUBONNET written on it.

Cherrylynn Resilio was the receptionist and the secretary for the firm, which was Tubby and his partner, Reggie Turntide. When she first came to work three years earlier she made it clear she expected to become indispensable, and she had succeeded. She had originally migrated, Tubby learned when he first interviewed her, from Seattle. She had eloped in the twelfth grade with a good-looking lumberjack and oil-field roustabout who had brought her to Louisiana to live in a brand-new trailer park in an overgrown sugar-cane plantation outside of New Iberia while he worked off-shore on the rigs, ten days on, seven days off. The seven days off must have been mainly strenuous partying because Cherrylynn just rolled her eyes, shook her head, and grinned when she told Tubby about that part of her past.

"We were a little crazy," she said, and smiled at Tubby like he must know what she meant. Actually, all he could do was imagine, and he knew that was probably a lot less fantastic than the real thing.

She didn't tell him what had caused the breakup exactly, but she had packed her suitcase and grabbed a Greyhound for New Orleans, looking for work. Tubby got the impression that her husband, or ex-husband—she was a little vague on that—could be in Texas, Louisiana, or Washington State for all she cared, but that she was apprehensive he might show up on her doorstep. Tubby did know that Cherrylynn kept her phone number unlisted.

Tubby had hired her, while Reggie was out of town, on the basis of her enthusiasm and desperation, not her experience, and he was real pleased with the way it had turned out. Admittedly, Cherrylynn was taking her time mastering legal-secretary–type things like preparing mortgage certificates, but she attacked filing, billing, and updating the Rolodex with a vengeance. She was also cute as a button in a windblown, wide-eyed, Puget Sound sort of way, and she made the clients feel at home.

Cherrylynn had already fixed her makeup and had her purse in her hand ready to leave for the day when Tubby walked in, but she immediately sat back at her desk.

"Here are your messages, Mr. Dubonnet," she said, handing the slips to Tubby. "Mr. Whiting called several times and said it was urgent. I put your letter to Mrs. Prado on your desk. Do you need me to stay?"

Jynx Margolis walked in just behind Tubby. She said hello to Cherrylynn and marched right past her into Tubby's office. Tubby smiled at Cherrylynn, who was not amused, and followed.

"I'd be glad to stay," Cherrylynn pleaded. Tubby waved goodbye to her and closed the office door.

His office was spacious, but the floor and most of the other flat surfaces were cluttered, as usual, with stacks of files. The walls were a soft pink, sort of a subdued violet, courtesy of building management, and a Persian rug covered most of the parquet floor. Two walls were glass, providing views of the French Quarter and the crescent of the Mississippi River. The third was covered by a bookcase, and along the fourth was a sofa nobody ever used except Tubby when he sometimes slept in right before trial. The furnishings were north Louisiana—a wide cypress desk from the office of a now defunct cotton compress, and comfortable upholstered chairs, purchased from a Shreveport undertaker when he retired. There were enough law books on the shelves to put new clients at ease. The rooftop swimming pool and tennis courts of the Fairmont Hotel were directly below. Tubby kept a telescope by his window focused on a well-positioned lounge chair by the pool.

Mrs. Margolis settled into one of the upholstered chairs facing the desk and began cooing over a framed photograph of one of Tubby's daughters.

"That's Debbie. She just turned twenty. Has her own apartment and everything. It's really great to see you, Jynx. You're looking just fantastic," he made a little contact with her bright eyes, "but I've got to be leaving soon." This wasn't really true, and Tubby wondered why he said it. Maybe because it made him sound important or maybe because the woman radiated a strong magnetic field that he instinctively tried to shield himself from for fear of getting helplessly polarized.

"Tubby, I think I'm going crazy. He's calling day and night."

"What does he say?"

"He curses at me. He says things like I'm a rotten mother, that I'm a cheap whore, that I'm sleeping with his best friend—what a joke that is—that he'll take the kids away. He only does it when he's been drinking, which he seems to be doing a lot of these days. I really should tape-record him and send it to the Boston Club."

"Maybe that's not a bad idea." Tubby looked at his watch but felt the pull. "Would you like a little drink yourself?" he asked.

"Yes," she said emphatically. She crossed her legs and found a cigarette in her purse. Tubby came around the desk and lit it, and then went to the miniature side bar concealed behind a closet door next to the sofa. He fixed her a gin and tonic, and a glass of tonic water with a slice of lime for himself.

She took a big sip and sighed happily. She leaned back in her chair, and her bosom rose and fell magnificently.

"These things reach a point of climax and taper off after a while," Tubby said soothingly. "You're at an emotional peak right now. Believe me. Everything is going to blow over and quit pounding on you soon." Better get back to business, he thought. "You've won the custody battle. He's not going to open up that whole soap opera of misdeeds again."

"He doesn't care about the kids. Now that we're dividing up the property, Byron's true colors have come out."

"He can't delay the process much longer, or keep his assets hidden unless he's a lot smarter than I think he is. I've got an investigator checking on his jewelry purchases. Everybody always leaves a trail." She had perfect café-au-lait skin, courtesy of extended weekends at Perdido Key and Destin. He could have studied any part of her for a long time. Her armpits, paler than the rest of her, were interesting. The faint brown wrinkles circling her knee caught his attention. The sandal straps starting up her ankle had a clever knot.

"I just want this to be over," Jynx said.

"You need to be patient," Tubby counseled. "It will take a while. Look after yourself. Take a trip."

"I suppose I do need to relax. It's very calming talking to you."

"You're good for the long haul, I know," Tubby said. "I hate to talk about money, but I must. My partner has been fussing at me for not collecting my unpaid bills. I'd appreciate it if you could make some sort of payment to cut the balance."

"Tubby," she said, putting her glass, emptied of all but a mashed lime, on his desk. "You know everything I have is tied up. The kids are literally eating the bank account. When we finally tag Mr. M, we can settle up on everything. But for now there's just little me against the world."

"Still I must be fair to my partner. There must be something you can do."

Jynx stood up and leaned over the desk. She stroked Tubby's face so gently he wasn't sure he had felt it. "You're the sweetest little lawyer in New Orleans," she said. "You've been patient and understanding from the beginning. When this is over, you'll get payment in full, I promise." A force moved him to cover her hand with his own. "Keep on looking out for me, Tubby," she whispered, her wounded brown eyes dissolving his.

Suddenly she straightened up. "Oh, naughty me." She waved goodbye on her way out the door.

Tubby stared for a few minutes at the empty space she had left. Then he finished his drink and tapped out the number of his ex-wife, Mattie. His middle daughter, Christine, answered.

"Hi, baby doll."

"Howya doin', Daddy?"

"What's happening?"

"Nothing much. We're going to Florida this weekend."

"Who's we?"

"Oh, me and some friends."

"Where?"

"Fort Walton."

"Oh, really?"

"Yes, Daddy. Mom's not home." He noticed how she changed the subject, but he let it pass.

"Where is she?"

"She had to go to the O'Briens' for cocktails by the pool."

"Is Collette in?" Collette was his youngest daughter.

"No, she's out."

"Where's that?"

"You know Collette. She's just out."

"How's school?"

"Great. Oh. There's another call coming in."

"Drive safe to Florida."

"I will."

"And tell your mother I called."

"I will."

"Love you."

"I love you, Daddy," she said, and switched him off.

Tubby went to the bar to pour himself another gin and tonic. This time he decided to leave out the tonic. He stood by the window and looked out over his city. He watched the lights of the barges below slowly plowing upstream in the river as it turned black in the gathering darkness.

Tubby recalled one particularly nice spring day. The family had gone for a picnic on the Bogue Falaya River, a sleepy little stream north of Lake Pontchartrain. They had towed the boat behind them across the Causeway while the morning fog was still clinging to the water. They got to the boat launch just when the sun broke through, a fuzzy yellow ball. Wisps of mist like smoke curled around the cypress knees by the bank and the pilings of the piers. When they got everybody packed, precariously, into the boat, along

with their barbecue grill, lawn chairs, and ice chest, they
puttered upstream to a low-water island. Collette jumped
in, waist deep, and pulled them onto the beach. With the
girls splashing around, and Mattie trying to keep her shorts
dry, they got everything unloaded. Mattie set about arrang-
ing the camp to her liking, and Tubby started the fire in
the grill. The girls all got back in the boat, and after fighting
over the wheel, let Debbie take them downstream toward
the deep water where they could go fast and ski.

Once the coals were lit and smoking, and the chairs were
all set up, he and Mattie settled down to relax. They had
about an hour to kill, and Tubby was thinking idly about
trying to interest Mattie in a little roll on the blanket she
had spread out on the sand. The setting was warm and very
serene. He dipped into the ice chest and popped open a can
of beer.

"You're drinking a little early," Mattie said, lighting a
cigarette.

"Hey, it's Saturday. It's a picnic."

"I don't want you falling asleep."

"Mattie, I'm not about to fall asleep." She had made him
uncomfortable all of a sudden. "Is anything bothering you?"
he asked.

She took a big pull on her cigarette and then held it with
her lips while she lifted up her hips and used both hands to
tug her shorts into a more comfortable position. A brown
hawk soared lazily overhead.

"Why do you always ask if something's bothering me?
Just because I ask about your drinking?"

Tubby took a stab at changing the subject. "Can you see
that turtle over there on that log?" He pointed across the

stream. "Do you know that they're called 'tarpins' in north Louisiana? They make it sound like the name of the big fish."

She didn't say anything, just dragged on her cigarette. Tubby tried to feel serene again, but couldn't.

"This is special, Mattie," he attempted. "What a beautiful place. Clean air, birds, old live oak trees with moss hanging off them like a pirate's lair, nothing to do but cook hot dogs, three gorgeous girls doing healthy things and baking like cookies on our very own boat. It's pretty nice, huh?"

"I hate it when you talk like that," she said quietly.

Tubby was annoyed. Could she be joking? "Are you nuts? What's the problem today, hon?"

"Nothing. It's just not enough. Anybody can lay out on the river, guzzling beer, and say isn't this great, but it's so common. There's more in the world than this, don't you think? There's more to it than being a turtle, sunning yourself on a log without any more to do than eat a bug."

"Like what?" Tubby asked.

"God, Tubby, like everything. Like Paris, stimulating people for a change, like cultural surroundings, like using your talents to their fullest."

"Jesus, Mattie. I didn't know you were so dissatisfied."

"I'm not dissatisfied. I feel like I'm in some kind of a vault I need to break out of."

"Maybe we should take a trip," he offered.

She was quiet for a while. Finally she said, "Don't worry about it. I'll be all right."

But he did worry about it, even after the girls came back in a storm of laughter and shouting about how each had done on the water skis and who from school they had seen out on the river. And it wasn't all right. It had just kept getting worse, and Tubby had felt more and more lost in his marriage until one day Mattie told him if he didn't move out and give her some space, she was going to go crazy. She threw and smashed enough things to be convincing, and Tubby had done as she said. It had possibly been a mistake, but he was used to it now.

SIX

At the beginning, it was half business, half romance, between Darryl and Monique. She did her job and got along with the rest of the staff. The crowd was mostly students and yuppies and boaters, and they basically drank a lot and tipped well. Waitresses wore tights and leather miniskirts. Behind the bar you wore black pants, a ruffled white shirt, and suspenders. Once or twice a week Darryl would pour her drinks when her shift ended at midnight, and they would go back to his office, or drive to his apartment a couple of blocks away, and have sex. They didn't go out much.

Sex with Darryl was very good for her. He was attentive and put a lot of himself into it, and he wasn't into anything that hurt, which was nice but took her a while to adjust to. Sometimes he would send her home in a cab, and sometimes they would sleep in each other's arms. She got accustomed to the way he smelled and liked it, like burnt toast.

* * *

Once Darryl set her up with a couple of customers after hours. He made a party of it, in the large private room upstairs from the bar, then let her know she was free to leave with them and charge whatever she could get. She didn't mind, and pocketed a couple of hundred bucks, but she was very nervous about how Darryl would feel about her afterward. It turned out he was okay, at least as far as she could see. They kept on dating after work, and she could tell he was falling for her though he saw some of the other girls, too. She moved from the French Quarter to a condo rental unit near the lake. Her old bike had been stolen when she left it on the street while she ran into a grocery store and forgot to lock it, so she bought a new one at Western Auto. She started riding it to work. Everyone said she was dumb to ride home around the lakefront by herself at night, but to her it was part of being the new and improved Monique, strong and brave.

Darryl still invited her upstairs to party every so often with some politicians or businessmen, nothing grungy, and he didn't complain when she went out with them, or when she turned them down. It was up to her. The only time he ever got really mad at her was when she once asked him if he would sell her a little cocaine. He went ballistic and almost got violent about it. He said he was no penny-ante dealer supplying the help and—his main point—if she wanted anything like that, all she had to do was ask and he would give it to her freely. How was she supposed to know that, she asked, and in so many words he said it was because he cared for her deeply. At least that was what Monique thought she heard him saying. She got extremely soft on him after that, and they became pretty much of a steady thing. He made her the head cocktail waitress and shift manager, and she more or less moved in with him. He didn't ask her to party with the customers much anymore, except one night with a particularly important pair of hot-shots, and she wished she'd said no to that.

It was the weekend before Mardi Gras Day, one of the high points of Carnival season and its zany final fortnight crammed with lavish public parades and private balls. The whole city had a crazy atmosphere. Champs was crowded all day. It was early March, but the weather was warm, springlike, and boats of all sizes tied up at the pier outside the bar for short stops. Drinkers moved noisily back and forth between deck and dockside, and when people, some of them masked, began rolling in off the streets after the parades passed, the joint really started jumping. It was intense, maintaining the steady flow of drinks, seeing that the bar was supplied, and keeping track of the waitresses who kept vanishing into the midst of the boisterous mob.

Monique was wired up when she turned her register over to Jimmy, the late-night manager who would pilot the place until it lost altitude and crashed to the ground around four or five in the morning. She had been sipping juice all night and had taken a little toot at around eight o'clock. Now she was quite ready for a couple of drinks. Her mind was on rest, not party, when she went upstairs to Darryl's office to take him the shift receipts.

His office was part of a large suite. To get there you passed through the private lounge furnished with a couch, card table, and chairs, and Darryl's guests used it to hang out in. When the club had live music the band had the run of the upstairs lounge to get stoked up and primed for their performance. The lights were kept very dim.

The nicest part about the room was that it opened onto a small balcony overlooking the lake and the boats tied up at the dock below. Monique noticed that there were people on the balcony when she walked past, but she didn't pay much attention to them. A hallway ran from the lounge past a bathroom, a small kitchen, and a locked storeroom and ended at the door of Darryl's office. It was also kept locked, whether he was inside or not, and it was covered by a security camera so that Darryl could know who was outside before he opened up. He buzzed Monique in. He was sitting facing away from her at his oak desk, counting money, and he nodded to her without looking up or losing count when she came in. He was wearing his regular late-night outfit, faded blue jeans and a baggy white-and-blue striped sweater, and his gold necklace and bracelet. The air conditioner was on high, and he had his big color television on for background noise. It was tuned in to Letterman.

"What a night," she said, placing her register tray on the desk.

"Still a good crowd?" he asked, without looking at her. He probably knew the answer anyway because there was a television monitor on the wall showing all the activity immediately around the bar.

"Huge," she said. "You want a drink?"

"Maybe in a minute. You help yourself."

Monique liked it better when Darryl poured, but she didn't say anything. She went to the bar and mixed up a concoction of orange juice, cranberry juice, and vodka. She took it to one of the garish vinyl-covered armchairs, plunked down, kicked off her sandals, and lit a cigarette. She leaned back and blew smoke, waiting for Darryl to finish the books.

"Was anybody out in the lounge?" he asked.

"I think there were a couple of guys out on the balcony. Are they all right?"

"They're not exactly all right, but it's cool. Are you busy tonight?"

"No." She thought it was polite of him to ask.

"Why don't you go out and get them some drinks. See what they want to do. They're looking for a good time."

"Who are they?"

"Just a couple of guys. They're from here. It would be good for business. You might like them."

"I'm pretty uptight."

"It's up to you. The big guy's probably loaded. Go see what they want to drink anyway."

"Okay." She put out her cigarette and got back up. She checked herself in the mirror and kissed the back of Darryl's neck. "Later for you, baby," she whispered in his ear. He smiled and gave her hand a squeeze but kept on tallying up the cash. She gave her hips a bounce when she walked out the door, thinking he might look around and see it.

There were two men on the balcony, partly hidden because one of the French doors was closed. She opened it when she went out. Both men were leaning over the rail, swapping jokes with some Loyola girls, according to their sweatshirts, sitting on the deck of a sailboat tied up below. The top of its mast was at their level, and they were trying to entice the girls to climb up. One of the men was skinny and looked like he might be a high school teacher or something. The other was built big and solid and had on a red nylon windbreaker.

"Care for anything to drink, gentlemen?" she asked.

They both looked around and checked her out.

"Whatever you're having," the big one said.

"About three fingers of Wild Turkey," said his partner.

"You got it," she told them, and went back inside. She called down to the bar on the house phone and asked Jimmy to send up the waiter with a beer and a whiskey and a cranberry juice for her. The big fellow followed her in and sat beside her on the couch. He offered her a Marlboro, which she accepted, and he lit it with a big butane lighter.

He asked her name and she told him. She asked his, and he said Jack Daniels. He was shitfaced already, she could tell. He had plenty of muscles, but he seemed to be in a good mood. He got cozy in stages, seeing what the rules were. A young waitress brought up the drinks, and he tipped her ten dollars from a roll. He had a lot of money and wanted Monique to know it. The slim man came off the balcony once to go back to the bathroom or maybe talk to Darryl. Monique couldn't tell where, but he was gone. Jack Daniels brought out a plastic pill bottle and tapped about a quarter teaspoon of white powder onto the card table.

"You want some of this?" he asked.

She said okay, and he played around with it for a minute with a small gold pocketknife, then they both sniffed some up through a rolled-up twenty. It was good stuff, and Monique completely spaced out. Jack Daniels got real friendly then and had his hands all over her while they talked and he shot the bull. She remembered that they ordered up more drinks. She kept enough of her wits about her to make him give her some money. He managed that without much of a break in the action. She asked what about his friend. Jack Daniels said something like he's just a fucking little old lady; he doesn't care about the finer things in life. They dipped into his pill bottle a couple more times. She jerked him off right on the couch. They went downstairs and had a drink. She remembered taking a ride out to the boat launch in his car. They did it in the backseat. He was a little too rough. She remembered he had a gun strapped to his chest. Put it together with the facts that he was big and muscular, with the beginnings of a beer belly, and she concluded, without too much brainwork, that he was a rogue cop. At least he came with all the trappings of cop-hood as she knew them. He dropped her off at her place and scratched off before she could find her keys.

Monique felt completely wrecked when she woke up late the next morning. After she finally got herself moving, she took her bike outside and rode all the way down Lakeshore Drive and back to try to clear her head. She reported to work a little early and tracked down Darryl to get a read on the situation. He acted like it was no big deal, nothing to forgive. Later on he mentioned that he was sorry he'd fixed her up like that. Those guys could be bad actors, he said. She should stay away from them. So what was she supposed to make of that?

Monique had a problem of her own. She had a prior conviction in Alabama—for possession with intent to sell. She had never told anybody in New Orleans about it. It was part of the degrading time of her life with Ned that she wanted to bury forever. She knew Darryl had a prior, too, but since he didn't talk about it, neither did she. It was one of the things they hadn't shared yet.

What's worse, she was still on probation. Except for her party nights, and except that she might keep a little grass or coke around for home consumption, she tried hard to stay clean. In other words, she didn't cut up much in public or do any dealing. She realized that Darryl did, but that was his affair and she kept out of it.

Sometimes Darryl would go away for a day or two, on business. It was none of hers. They weren't married. He sometimes made her wait in the hall for a few minutes before buzzing her into his office, and he had even once sent her outside while he took a phone call. She was naturally curious but not too concerned. She didn't think that it involved another woman, and that was the main thing that scared her. She hadn't seen anything serious develop in that area, though. Darryl might sleep around a little, but he showed her enough respect to hide it well. That was something she appreciated. She had fallen in love with Darryl, she believed. She liked the way he ran things, the way he was casual around drugs, the way his mood always stayed up no matter what trouble he'd had. She could visualize finally starting to build a home base. The air by the lake was fresh and clean, and wet breezes flushed away the blue fog she got in her mind from working behind a bar. She was making good money, enough to send some regularly home to her mama to help care for Lisa.

Lisa, the child she had had with Ned, was another of the things she hadn't yet revealed to Darryl. Lisa stayed with

Monique's mama in Evergreen. She was four years old, and she wrote letters to Monique, the kind that little girls write. The arrangement had begun when Monique had been arrested and spent a little time in Atmore at what they called a rehabilitation center. Monique's mama hadn't quite gotten over that, and she still wouldn't let Monique visit Lisa. Monique imagined that she and Darryl might get married, and then he would help her get Lisa back no matter what her mama said.

The closest she or Darryl came to talking about kids was when she asked him if he had any brothers and sisters. No, he said, he was an only child.

"Where did you grow up?" she asked.

"Mostly here in New Orleans," he said. "My father sent me and my mother here to live in an apartment when I was a little boy. When I got out of high school, he told my mother to come home and left the apartment to me."

"Where did he live?"

"In Mexico City."

"What did he do?"

"He had a shoe factory," Darryl said, looking right in her eyes in a way that said he didn't want to talk about it.

"You had an apartment and lived all by yourself?"

"That's right."

"I grew up with lots of kids myself. Mama had four girls and one boy."

"That must have been nice."

"It was, most of the time. I like a big family."

"Didn't you fight a lot?"

"You better believe it. But we always made up."

"In my family, everybody got their own pork chop. That's

one thing I remember my father used to say. We didn't have to fight over them, you see?"

"Weren't you ever lonesome?"

"Not really. I played with myself." Darryl laughed.

"I can't imagine having a family without a lot of kids," she said, trying to get him back on track.

He didn't reply, and she had to let it drop.

Monique rode her bicycle down to the blue mailbox to send Lisa a postcard of the monkeys in the Audubon Zoo. She had written that someday the two of them would visit the zoo together. There was a danger, of course, that her mama would throw the card away, but Monique couldn't help that. She was pedaling back to her apartment when the driver of a parked car swung his door open, almost causing her to crash into it head first. She had to slide off the seat and put both feet on the ground to stop. She turned on the driver with her mouth open and a yell halfway out, when she saw it was "Jack Daniels," the guy Darryl had told her to stay away from a couple of months before.

"Oh, so sorry, Monique," he said, grinning. He didn't look sorry, and he looked even more like a cop in the daytime than he did when he was stoned at night. Big guy, long sideburns, giving off asshole, macho vibes. Ned, her ex, had been a small-town cop, giving her an attitude about cops in general, but evidently something about them attracted her, too—a mystery she was trying to work out.

"I thought it was time maybe we had another date," Jack Daniels said.

"That's a crazy way to ask for it. You could have broken my neck. And, since you asked, I don't think so."

"Come on, baby. Didn't I prove I was a nice guy? I've been missing you."

"Sorry, I don't go in for reruns. It sends the wrong message."

"I liked the message you sent the first time."

"It will just have to last you." Monique started to back up on her bike to get away from there.

"Don't leave me yet," he said. "Are you getting all the nose candy you want?"

"That was just one time, Mr. Jack Daniels. And, yeah, I get everything I need."

"I'm sure your probation officer would like to hear that."

She stopped and stared at him. He was still grinning with a real sincere look in his eyes.

"What are you talking about?" she asked.

"I'm talking about J. W. Whitley, your probation officer in beautiful Brewton, Alabama, honey, and how you're violating those important rules he told you about. It's all in the national crime computer, plain as day. I'm talking about tossing your apartment and busting you, little girl. I'm talking about sending you back to Alabama."

This can't be happening, Monique thought, but I can handle this.

"I don't know what you're talking about," she spat out. "I've got friends here. Talk to my lawyer. I don't need to listen to your bullshit."

"Yeah you do, Monique. Ever since our little affair together, I've been asking around about you. I know you're Darryl Alvarez's special squeeze, though the way he treats you I personally don't understand. And I've talked to, wanna guess? Neddy. Ol' Officer Ned of the Evergreen, Alabama, PD? He wants custody of a little girl named Lisa. I think when I bust you and send you back that will be very easy for him."

A black hole opened up underneath Monique and she fell in. It closed up on top and all the sunlight was gone. It was all darkness and cold, in there, inside her head.

She stared at the man and tilted her head to one side.

"What do you want?" she asked. She really had no idea what it could be, what could come out of his mouth, that she didn't want to hear.

"Your man, Darryl, is taking a drive down to the Gulf sometime in the next week or two. I want to know when."

"I don't have any idea what you're talking about."

"Better make it your business to find out. I need to know exactly when he's going."

"And then what?"

"And then you call me and ask for Casey. Here, I'll write it down." He scribbled on the inside of a matchbook cover: *Casey, 555-3233.*

"What do you want to know for?"

"It's business. But nothing happens to Darryl. He'll be fine. Don't you worry. We'll talk some more later."

He started the car. "Watch out you don't get run over," he laughed, and pulled away from the curb while she frantically yanked her bike out of the way.

Instead of going back to her apartment, Monique rode way out to the end of the rock jetty that protected the boats in the harbor. The day had turned cloudy and windy, and whitecaps rolled across the lake. Most of the sailors were back in, and the stragglers were tacking hard in her direction. A couple of boys on jet skis carved circles through the waves and blasted through the air in earsplitting two-stroker ecstasy. She stayed on the rocks for a long time letting the wind and lake spray blow over her. The water tasted sad. Warm and a little salty, like tears. It was hard to sort things out. She thought about running away again. Back to Alabama, grab Lisa, and then, where? It had taken so much energy to get here, to this little spot in New Orleans. It was very depressing to imagine leaving everything behind and doing it all again.

Monique couldn't come to any decision out on the rocks. Except she decided to hope that she never heard from Mr. Casey again, that she never saw him, that he never telephoned. She didn't know what he was talking about anyway. And he had promised that no harm would come to Darryl. So what could he want?

Monique went back to work and didn't say anything. Everything ran smoothly for two days. She began to calm down and think maybe nothing was going to happen.

Then Darryl brought her into it. After her shift ended on the third day following her talk with Casey, she carried her receipts up to the office as usual. When Darryl finished with the books they often had a few drinks, maybe smoked a joint, and decided whether they would go to his place, her place, or each to their own place.

"Baby," he said. "I'd like you to help me with something. It's a big one."

He sounded very serious, so she gave him her full attention. She was ready to do anything he wanted.

"Whatever you say, honey. Just ask. You know that."

It was a big one. The idea was that Darryl was going to

drive a truck down to the boonies on Sunday night. He wanted her to follow him in his Mazda. She would be carrying something. At a certain spot she would park and wait while he went about his business. It might be forty-five minutes. Then, when he called her on the car phone, she would come on and meet him.

"It's that simple." Darryl spread his hands to show her that was all there was to it.

"I really hate to ask you," he said, "but there's nobody else I trust."

Monique felt terrible.

That was on a Thursday. Thinking about Darryl's trip tormented Monique so much that she stayed home from work the next night. She huddled up in her bed and watched television, trying not to think any thoughts, and drinking wine coolers till she really did feel ill.

Casey the cop called on Saturday morning.

"You're missing work. What's going on?"

"Nothing," she said. "I'm just sick. Are you watching me?"

"You bet. And I know something's cooking. When is Darryl taking a trip?"

"I don't know. Leave me alone," she sniffled.

Casey got loud. He threatened her and went over her options. One, she could be the subject of an intense police investigation. Casey was stretching things here. He had some pals on the NOPD who might knock on her door and ask about the aroma of dope if he called them, but they wouldn't stick their necks out too far for free. Two, he could arrange it so that someone else, not him personally of course, beat the living shit out of her. That would be a good job for Freddie, or he could even tap Bin Minny, but then he'd have to cut the big guy in. Third, he would let her mother and everybody in Evergreen know that Monique was a coke-snorting hooker in a New Orleans bar so that even little Lisa would be afraid of catching some disease from her. Four, all of the above.

Or, she could tip him off and he wouldn't bother her anymore.

Freddie, listening to Casey's end of this conversation at BB Bonds, got so excited he jumped out of his chair and punched the air.

"I'm not going to leave you fucking alone," Casey told Monique. "I'm going to be on you like a fly on shit until you tell me when the fuck Darryl is taking his trip."

"He doesn't let me know that stuff," she bluffed, but Casey knew from the way she said it that she was lying.

"Bitch—listen to what I'm telling you. There's nobody standing between you and me. I'm your bad dream. This is the law talking. I'm going to come down there and whip your ass and bust your ass all the way back to Alabama."

"Go away, you bastard," she cried.

Casey was quiet for a moment. Then he said, softly, "You are not going to deny me or get past me. I'm going to see that you do time in some really terrible joint. Where, it doesn't matter. And I'm going to personally see to it that your little baby girl has an extremely sick and warped child-hood."

She couldn't hold out after that. It took just a couple of seconds for her to tell him that Darryl had said something about taking a ride on Sunday. She didn't tell him where Darryl was going, that she would be going along, or anything else. Casey poked a little more, but he was satisfied. It would be easy to trail Darryl. He'd been promised the cooperation of certain people in the DEA, and those guys had radar, helicopters, the works. This was turning out to be a piece of cake.

After Casey hung up, Monique prayed to the telephone that it would all work out okay. He had said no harm would come to Darryl. Would he lie? There was no way she was going to tell Darryl what she had done. She crossed her knees like a yogi and closed her eyes. She put her mind on hold and let winds of guilt and fear whip around her. She finally calmed down enough to turn on the TV and fall asleep.

SEVEN

O<small>N</small> SUNDAY MORNING,
bright and early, Tubby picked up his youngest daughter,
Collette, for church. It was something they had been doing
together for a month now, motivated by Collette. Tubby
wasn't sure why a fourteen-year-old girl had a renewed interest in church attendance, but it was more than all right
with him. Other girls her age were smoking crack and
dropping out of school. If she wanted to join the Young
Republicans he would pay the dues, though his upstate
relatives had voted Democrat since before the war. The
services were relaxing, too. The organ music and the rituals
smoothed out his mental wrinkles, and he wondered why
he had not bothered to come for so many years. It filled up
a day that was often empty of late.

At the conclusion of the service, after shaking hands with
the priest and promising to come back, they walked over to
Audubon Park and took a stroll around the lagoon. It was
a pretty morning, and they shared the pathways with joggers

and Rollerbladers in colorful attire and young mothers, in pairs, giving their Newman-bound babies some air.

They went down to the graveled edge of the pond to watch a small boy feed the ducks. A fat old drake with muddy feet boldly waddled over to them to investigate the food possibilities. Collette tossed a dandelion in its direction. It pecked the flower, then made a clumsy departure.

"Do these ducks live here, or are they just passing through?" she asked.

"The white ones live here. I think the ones with the green heads are migrating. They're probably very happy to find a place where nobody is shooting at them."

"Who would shoot such pretty birds?" she mused to herself.

Tubby didn't remind her about his own hunting trips.

"What are you doing this afternoon?" he asked. He was thinking he might invite her to go to the movies or go skating or something.

"Mom and I are going shopping for a prom dress. My prom is Friday night."

"You can't have a prom in the eighth grade," he said.

"Of course we do." Obviously a stupid statement.

"Who are you going with, Jeffrey?" That was a safe bet. She had been friends with Jeffrey for years. He was a Ben Franklin student. And he had a driver's license.

"Yes, there are four of us going together. It's all very well organized and properly chaperoned." She had the bases covered.

"Well, call me if you need anything."

"You mean, like, money?"

"Heck no, not money."

"What else would I need?"

"You never can tell."

"Oh, you mean like the time you rescued Debbie?"

"Yeah," he laughed. "Something like that."

He had been at a deposition. His client had been in the "hot seat." For some reason, either because the opposing attorney was from out of town or because there was a hearing set for the next day—Tubby couldn't remember—they were holding the deposition after hours. The issue was a commercial real-estate transaction gone sour. The plaintiff thought Tubby's client—who was Monster Mudbug's father—had promised to sell him a building, then broken his word and sold it to someone else. He believed he was aggrieved by all the profits he would have made if he had been able to purchase the building, then tear it down and put up a hotel. It was dragging along past nine o'clock, and the questioning from opposing counsel, Bob Thomas, had degenerated into something like:

"I'll show you Deposition Exhibit Four. This is Branscomb's letter to you dated August second. I'll ask you to look at it."

"Okay," said Tubby's client.

"Do you remember it?"

"Sort of. It looks like a million other letters."

"Did you have any discussions between Exhibit Three and Exhibit Four—with Branscomb, that is? Think hard and tell me."

"What are you saying?" the witness asked.

"Wait," Tubby cut in. "Objection that the question is too confusing to follow and is not even a question."

"I don't know what he means," Adrian's father said to

the court reporter, like perhaps she could explain it. She faithfully took down every word, smiling at him sympathetically while she did so.

"Maybe you could put all those letters in a row on the table," Tubby suggested, "and we could all understand better what you are asking about."

"I'm trying to be precise," Thomas said in exasperation, "and I'll ask that you resist the temptation to interrupt at every question."

"I'm not interrupting," Tubby protested hotly. "I'm objecting, and it's not a temptation, it's my responsibility as this man's lawyer."

Before Tubby could get on a roll with his speech, the telephone in the conference room rang, and the court reporter was distracted. Tubby took a deep breath and went to the credenza to pick it up. It was his answering service, and a woman told him that his daughter was on the line.

"Put her through," he said.

"Hello, Daddy? This is Debbie." He remembered that it was Debbie's first prom—not at her own school but at her date's. Tubby had asked Mattie to be sure to get a picture of her in her gown—parenting by proxy.

"Hi, Debbie. What's wrong?"

"Can you come get me?"

"Why—where are you?"

"I'm at the Marriott. I'm stranded. Josh got drunk and drove off, and I don't know anybody here, and I'm very upset."

"Sure, honey. Can you take a cab?"

"I don't have any money with me. I called home already but nobody answered."

"Are you in the lobby?"

"Yes," she snuffled.

"Go out by the front door, where the doorman in the red coat is standing. I'll pick up the car and be around in about ten minutes."

"Thank you, Daddy."

Tubby hung up and got his coat.

"Sorry. Illness in the family. We're going to have to reconvene at a later date."

"What? You can't do that," the opposition insisted.

"Let's go," Tubby said to his client, who also got up and grabbed his smokes.

"My apologies, counselor, family emergency," Tubby said.

"What is this? Is somebody in the hospital? What's going on?" Thomas sputtered.

"Can you show him the way out, please?" Tubby asked the court reporter. "And please turn off the lights."

"Yes, sir," she said.

"Goodnight, everybody," Tubby said as he went out the door with his client in tow.

In the elevator Adrian's father said, "That was a neat trick, Tubby. He was getting me all mixed up. You want to go catch a couple of drinks?"

"No, really, Sid. I have to go pick up my daughter. She got marooned at the prom."

"Hey, whatever works."

That's how you got a reputation as a smart lawyer.

Quacking and beating the air frantically with their wings, the ducks scattered away from a huge Labrador retriever who splashed happily into the lagoon. The birds settled into the water a few yards away and then led the snorting beast, his head sticking out of the pea green water, in circles around and around the pond.

"Anyhow, call me if you need me," Tubby told Collette.

That Sunday night Monique followed Darryl across the Mississippi on the Huey P. Long Bridge. Monique, behind the wheel of the Mazda, had never been this way before, and she was thrilled to be so high up, like riding a Ferris wheel. The chemical plants and shipyards far below lit up the river like the midway of a carnival she had been to as a child. After they got across and were pointed southwest on Highway 90, Darryl instructed her, on the car phone, to slow down and let him get about a mile ahead. He asked if she was doing all right, and she said yes. She really did feel good. It was an adventure. Darryl had tossed a blue gym bag in the backseat. That was what she was supposed to bring him later.

Darryl had installed a fantastic Sony compact disc player in the car, and she listened to Garth Brooks and Willie Nelson. She smoked cigarettes and tapped the wheel with her nails. The Rex and Endymion beads hanging on the rearview mirror danced back and forth. Darryl checked in every five minutes or so when he saw something interesting. He pointed out a restaurant he said the Mafia owned, and when they drove through a swamp he told her to look out for alligators, you might see the car lights reflected in their eyes. He also asked if she saw anybody following them. She hadn't really been paying any attention, but she told him no. After that she started checking her mirror, but she didn't know how you could tell one pair of headlights from another.

They drove through the town of Houma, on the bypass, and then turned left onto a narrow blacktop running in a direct line south, to the sea. It was dark, but Monique could tell that the land they were passing through was perfectly flat. Darryl told her it was nothing but rice fields and marshes. The flashing lights in the far distance could be oil rigs out on the Gulf, he said, or maybe power lines or boats. Finally he said he was pulling over, and in a minute she saw his lights off to the side. He was idling behind a trash Dumpster in what looked to be the middle of nowhere. She crushed onto the gravel and pulled in beside him.

Darryl got out of the truck and came around, and she rolled down her window.

"I'm going down about five miles," he said. "You come to a place where this road makes a T almost. The main road hooks off to the right, and there's another road that goes left. It's gravel. It goes to some fishing camps, maybe two miles down the road. When I call you, just drive down there and meet me. Remember, straight to the fork. Turn off left. Come to me, two miles. When you leave, just go out the way you came in. You're just bringing me the bag. Don't hang around. Don't get out of the car. Nobody needs to see you. I'll call in about an hour. You got it? Can you wait that long?"

Monique nodded. "I live for you," she said.

Darryl's eyebrows seemed to pinch together, and his eyes twitched a little bit. "You're the one, Monique," he said, and kissed her. "Just do like I told you."

He winked at her and got back in the truck. She cut off her lights and engine. Darryl rolled off, and in a couple of minutes the sound of his motor disappeared. Monique was all alone on a slender bridge of asphalt in the center of a million miles of marsh grass, salt air, and the biggest, blackest sky she could ever remember seeing. There were some stars, but no moon. It was so quiet she became conscious of the sound of her own breathing. Then some night insects, or frogs, began croaking at one another, and a mosquito hummed into the car. Something rustled around in the Dumpster. Maybe a raccoon, she thought. It sounded bigger than a raccoon. She rolled up the window quickly, put Juanita Judd on the Discman, and smoked. She kept checking her watch.

Because she had the music on, Monique didn't hear the car coming. It raced past with its headlights off, and scared the bejeezus out of her. Right behind it came two more cars, whoosh, whoosh, no lights. It was black as coal outside, but she thought she saw bubble-gum machines on top. She immediately killed the stereo and slumped down in the seat. The night swallowed the sounds of the car engines, and it became as quiet as the inside of a coffin. She chewed off most of her fingernails. The phone didn't beep. She waited an hour, and then some.

When she couldn't stand it anymore she started the car up and backed out onto the roadway. She thought for a moment about going straight back to New Orleans, but she couldn't just desert Darryl, so she turned to the right. She kept her lights off, too. Nobody was coming, and the road went straight as a bullet. After driving five minutes she reached the T and stopped to look around. Way down the gravel road she could see lights, flashing blue ones and one steady bright white one, like she had seen on a movie set once on Canal Street. They might have been a couple of miles away, but you didn't need to be a rocket scientist to figure out what was going on.

Monique jammed the shifter into the slot marked "R" and peeled out backwards. She pointed the Mazda due north and mashed the gas pedal down flat.

She got back home in a lot less time than the trip out had taken. After riding around her block, looking for things suspicious, she parked the car and ran into her apartment carrying the blue bag, which she pushed under her bed. Then she sat in front of the TV, rocking back and forth with her arms tight around her knees. There was no one she could call.

Monique woke up at around noon on Monday, got dressed, and went over to the restaurant. The bartender, a guy named Larry, filled her in on the news. Darryl had been busted down in the bayou. Larry didn't know too many details yet, but it had made the radio. She tried to act as though she was extremely shocked. She made a scene about being upset, then drove back to her apartment in the Mazda and waited. She was preparing to go to work at four o'clock when the phone finally rang.

"Hey, babe," he said. He sounded really tired.

"Hi, honey. Where are you?"

"In jail. The good officer here is letting me make a phone call."

"Are you all right?"

"Oh yeah," he sighed. "I'm fine. Here's what I need you

to do. I want you to go to the safe in the office and take out fifteen thousand dollars. There should be that much there. Give it to Jimmy. It's for my bail. He'll know what to do. He ought to have me home by tomorrow."

She liked the way he said "home."

"Have you got my car in a safe place?" he asked.

"Yeah. It's parked right outside. Everything is okay."

"All right. I'll see you tomorrow."

"I'll be here," she told him.

Darryl was naturally bummed out about his bust, but Monique sensed that he was also trying to figure something out. She could tell the pieces weren't fitting right. He was back at work at Champs, but he was very distracted. All of the employees told him how sorry they were, and he told them to forget about it. Everything would work out. The bar still did good business, the same as always, but the guys in suits, the ones Darryl always called "the players," disappeared completely. The phone in the office stopped ringing.

Darryl started drinking a little bit more.

"When this is all over, let's take a trip," Monique suggested.

"Where would you like to go?"

"Oh, I don't know. Canada, maybe."

"What's in Canada?" he asked.

"Wouldn't it be fun to go someplace really different? I'd like to see the Yukon, and the Mounties with the red coats."

"It's really cold up there."

"I don't think it would be too cold in the summertime. They have to be able to pan for gold, like you see in the movies, so you know the water can't be frozen all the time. Have you ever been?"

"No," Darryl said.

"Well, I'd like to go."

"Suits me," he said. "We can celebrate me getting out of prison."

"You're not going to have to go to prison, are you?"

"Being realistic, Monique, it's a possibility."

"Were you in before?"

"When I got busted?"

"Yes."

"Just for a couple of months. It was one of their so-called nice places, up near Monroe."

"Was it real hard for you?"

"No, just boring. You see some shitty things happen inside, though. You got to stay on your toes to keep out of trouble. You hear as little as possible, you know what I mean. I guess it's hard to imagine if you've never been there."

It was an opening, but Monique didn't take it. They were at Darryl's apartment, and Monique tried to comfort him with hugs and kisses. He was so listless that it took some time to get his motor running. Trying in the only way she knew to make things up to him, she told him to lie back and forget his troubles. She slipped off her dress and knelt over him, gently trailing her hair over his face and chest, letting his hands roam over her body until he was aroused.

Lying in his big bed afterward, sharing a cigarette, Darryl started up again. "Did you ever wonder what it feels like to be on the moon?" he asked.

She asked him what he meant.

"Just circling around in orbit. No communication. Lost in space, but under the control of something bigger than you. You can't get away from it, and you can't get any closer to it."

She didn't know how to respond, so she said, "Yeah, I kind of know what you mean."

"It's really weird," was all the comment Darryl would make. She squeezed his shoulder to encourage him, but he was finished.

Still, he seemed to have it under control. He would tell jokes and make the customers laugh.

He came over to Monique's apartment and got the blue bag about a week after his arrest. First he opened it up and gave her $50,000 in cash. That was for her to hold on to, he said. It was money to take care of herself with, hire lawyers, or whatever she might need or he might want.

The sight of all that cash really upset her. She grabbed Darryl with both hands and tried to shake him, though he was too big to shake.

"I need to know what we're into here," she shouted in his face. She wasn't thinking when she said "we," but Darryl picked up on it. He looked at her funny and sat on the bed. He took her hand.

"It really was stupid for me to get you involved," he said. He fumbled around for a cigarette, as usual.

"I don't care about that. I just want to know what's really going on." She took one of his hands in both of hers.

He ran his fingers through his thick black hair. "I'm not sure what I can tell you, babe. Something definitely went wrong. I was supposed to be protected. It was arranged for the Terrebonne Parish deputies to be somewhere else. I've done this before, and there's never been a problem. But all of a sudden the place is full of federal men. I don't know how they found out about it, but it was just them at first. When the local law showed up later they were almost apologetic about the whole thing. But at the start it's just these federal yo-yo's, and they were so interested in me they lost the boat. It just backed up and gunned out of there as soon as the cars with the blue flashers rolled in. You'd have thought they could have stopped it down the bayou, but they didn't. Maybe they were shorthanded. This one cop, he has on no uniform, he keeps pushing and shoving me, getting right in my face, going, 'Where's the money?' He kept yanking me around saying, 'Where's the cash?' He didn't care at all about any drugs. 'Give me the cash. It's your ticket out of here,' he was saying. And there was a guy in one of the cars who never did get out. I couldn't see who he was. Him and the guy who was hassling me drove away while the DEA federales were still taking pictures of the pot.''

"And all the time the money was with me," Monique said.

"Yeah, good thing."

"Who does it belong to?"

"You don't want to know. Hey, maybe it's mine now."

EIGHT

REGGIE TURNTIDE WAS slightly built, had thinning hair, wore square, tinted wire rims, and maintained a good tan. The glasses were mostly for effect. He liked to polish them, or twirl them around, or suck on one of the earpieces while he was talking to a client. Reggie had a lot of hustle, but he was never seen in court. His favorite clients were local and state politicos, and the kind of people who hung around them, and he had made his reputation in zoning permits, municipal ordinances, and state construction regulations. He had a keen eye for the fine line dividing permitted public profiteering from outright fraud, and he got paid to show it to his clients before they heard it from the state attorney general.

Reggie liked to say he complemented Tubby. Rarely did their work overlap. They had started off as social friends, through their wives, before they had been law partners. What Tubby liked about Reggie was his gift for gab and his unshakable cynicism. Reggie could walk into any room full of people and find hands to shake. He would have been naturally suited to politics if he hadn't thought it was beneath him. He liked to be the guy who put things together, and he was out for bigger game—bigger money—than public office offered, even in Louisiana, where it offered a lot.

The only time Tubby had ever seen Reggie nonplussed was when they were both in moot court back in law school. The occasion was a trial—not a real one but a student enactment to learn from experience the feel of the courtroom—but the judge's role was being played by an honest-to-God federal judge named Sealey, whose teaching method was to kick ass. Tubby was one of the jurors, and Reggie was the defense attorney. When time came for his opening statement, Reggie came from behind his counsel table and approached the jury. As the words, "Ladies and gentlemen of the jury," came out of his mouth, he lazily took off his jacket—with visions, no doubt, of a folksy William Jennings Bryan clouding his senses. Judge Sealey's eyes bugged out. Reggie popped his suspenders and got no further than, "This case is about greed," when the judge began pounding his gavel on the bench, like there was a rattlesnake he wanted dead and bellowed, "Young man, turn around."

Reggie complied so swiftly that he almost tripped and had to brace himself against the jury box for support. Great circles of perspiration suddenly appeared on his shirt.

"You will never," shouted the judge, "never, never, take off your coat in my courtroom. If you ever seek to practice in my courtroom again without your coat on, I will cite you for contempt and have you ejected by the bailiff." Never mind that there was no bailiff present among the dramatis personae; the point was made. Reggie dove for his coat and got into it posthaste.

"You may continue," the judge said, mildly. And Reggie did, in a weak voice, but he kept it short. He never repeated the mistake. In fact, Tubby noticed that over the years, you hardly ever saw Reggie without a coat, a blazer, or at least a sweater covering his shoulders. If he was caught somewhere where it would look odd, like on a beach or a golf course, Reggie might let his shirtsleeves show, but he seemed ill at ease when he did.

Tubby and Reggie rarely crossed paths after graduation, since Tubby concentrated on trial work and Reggie was generally allergic to courtrooms. They kept track of each other through their wives, who were both active in the Friends of the New Orleans Museum of Art. The Pan Am airplane crash in Kenner brought them back together professionally.

Reggie had inserted himself into the plaintiffs' team, though he made no pretense—to the other lawyers at least—that he knew anything whatsoever about personal injury law. One of the bereaved families—there were about two hundred of them—had hired Reggie, due to some misunderstanding of his competence, which gave him the right to sit at the counsel table. He immediately began organizing the lawyers, moderating such questions as to how to apportion shares of the recovery and who would do the actual work, and negotiating with insurance companies. Whenever there is money in the parish, the politicians get theirs, and Reggie helped to cut up and serve that piece of the soufflé, too. Inspired by the proximity of their husbands, the wives arranged a dinner together, and then a lake trip, and everybody became friends. When the complicated financial settlement was finally reached, Reggie did very well. As did Tubby, who actually put in a lot of courtroom hours and handled several depositions and witnesses. Over drinks at the celebration dinner in the Rex Room at Antoines, beneath the framed portraits of past Carnival royalty going back through decades of civic service, the two victors decided to throw in together.

Since Tubby's and Mattie's divorce, however, they hardly ever saw each other after hours, but they got along fine as partners. They didn't argue about money, but split it all. Tubby sometimes thought Reggie got the better of the deal, just because he never saw Reggie working very hard. But he had a talent for bringing in the business. And, to be honest, Reggie was better at collecting his bills than Tubby was. Whenever a new client found the firm, Reggie would smile and say, "Pennies from heaven," and he would keep smiling till they fell.

This morning Reggie was in Tubby's office wanting to talk about Darryl Alvarez, a client he had given to Tubby. Darryl, Tubby knew, was the manager of a bar at the lakefront and always had plenty of cash. He flashed it for lots of politicos and Jefferson Parish real-estate developers, who all loved Darryl, and since Reggie hung out with the same group of pals, he loved Darryl, too. Darryl was great for free meals, tickets to Saints games at the Dome, and tips on horse races. He also made a *buena* margarita. But, Reggie had sadly told Tubby a couple of weeks before, Darryl had a problem.

He had been caught with a new Ford wide-body pickup

truck in Terrebonne Parish, unloading fifteen bales of marijuana from a shrimp boat. Where it had started its journey
was anybody's guess, but it ended with Darryl staring into
a DEA agent's spotlight. He called Reggie from the Parish
Jail. Reggie, like most of Darryl's buddies, suddenly didn't
want to know him at all, but he did at least wake Tubby
up at home. Tubby drove down early in the morning. It
took a while, but he eventually got the bond lowered from
its initial million dollars to a measly $150,000. By some
means Tubby never learned about, Darryl got a bondsman
to post the bail, and he was soon back in his nightclub.

Reggie wanted to know how Darryl's case was coming,
and Tubby told him.

"I offered Fred Stanley, the U.S. Attorney, five years,
simple possession, but he laughed. He's trying for life.
What he wants is for Darryl to turn around."

"Turn around on whom?"

"I don't know. I guess whoever he bought the pot from.
He hasn't told me."

"No chance of getting him off?"

"He's working on the 'It was my twin brother' defense,
and the 'I thought it was hay for a Halloween hayride'
defense. So far no takers."

"I appreciate your handling this, Tubby. Has he been
paying you?"

"No problem there. He's ahead of the game. When he
comes in this afternoon I may ask for another deposit."

"That's great." Reggie did his little finger-flutter, taken
from the "itsy-bitsy spider," meaning here comes more
manna from the sky.

"These pennies ain't from heaven," Tubby said.

Reggie laughed and was still chuckling merrily when he went off down the hall toward his office. Defending Darryl did not bother Tubby. He had always liked the kid, too.

Darryl came by after lunchtime, which for Tubby had been fried oysters on French with melted butter and lemon juice. Cherrylynn had bought it at The Pearl down the street. Tubby ate the sandwich, all fourteen inches of it, at his desk, brushing the crumbs off a Memorandum in Support of Exception of Vagueness he was reading. He wondered how Californians got by on raspberry yogurt or Whoppers or whatever it was they ate for lunch.

Darryl came in carrying a blue gym bag, the kind a lot of people now showed off to suggest that they had spent their lunch hour working out at an executive spa. Despite his wavy black hair and the two gold chains around his neck, Darryl did not look so hot. A little frayed, maybe. But he flashed his big smile when he asked, "How's it going today, Tubby?"

"I'm staying busy. Have a seat." Darryl was pretty fidgety. Maybe facing prison time did that to you. Tubby told him about his talk with the U.S. Attorney.

"You think they've got a case?" Darryl asked.

"I don't see how a first-year law student could miss landing you, Darryl. All they've got to do is show the videotape of you waving at the camera with your hand on a ton of marijuana while a shrimp boat disappears into the Gulf. I'm just giving you the straight poop. They misspelled a few words in the indictment, but I don't think that's going to save you. They read you your rights four times. If you don't want to take the hit, you're going to have to tell them what you haven't told me. Who were you selling it to? Or, who were you working for?"

Darryl sighed. "If I told you that, I'd have a lot more problems than I have now. So what are we talking about if I get convicted?"

"The penalty for possession of that much pot with intention to sell is a minimum of twenty-five years, up to life. Except for your little cocaine bust in 1985, this is your only offense. Because I'm such a good lawyer, I think you'll get the twenty-five years and serve about eight."

Darryl sighed again. "Monique would shit over that."

"Who is Monique?" Tubby asked.

"Aw, she's my girlfriend. We're probably getting married. She's my night manager at Champs. I told her I might have to do six months. I think she might get another job if I got eight years."

"Give me something to tell the U.S. Attorney and let's make a deal. Then everybody's happy."

"Not as happy as you might think," Darryl muttered. "I'll see if maybe the Governor will commute my sentence. I contributed enough."

"Not even the Governor can commute a federal sentence. He just can't reach over to Pensacola and say, 'You've got one of my very best friends locked up in your very comfy prison. Please cut him loose and send him home to the 'Gret Stet' of Louisiana.' "

"No? Okay, I guess not. What happens next?"

"I'm going to file discovery motions and see what the rest of their evidence is—other than catching you with several bales of grass in your truck. They'll set it for trial in September, October maybe. There's not much for you to do now but look after your business. And maybe you should take a little time off and spend it with Monique."

"I've been thinking about doing that, too. Maybe run over to Gulf Shores or, who knows, fly up to Canada."

"Whereabouts in Canada?"

"Heck if I know. Monique says she wants to go to the Yukon and see the Mounties." Darryl shook his head. "Listen Tubby, could I leave this with you?" He plunked the gym bag down on Tubby's desk. The way he lifted it made it look heavy. "It's important that it be in a safe place."

"What is it?" Tubby didn't want to touch it.

"It's a lot of my business records. And some personal stuff to do with Monique. I've been getting things organized for going away, and this is stuff I don't want to leave lying around. I was thinking you probably got some room in your safe. I wouldn't want to leave it here more than a week. After that, I've made other arrangements."

"Let me see what's in it."

"I don't want to open it, Tubby, and I don't think you want to see this stuff. I swear it's just papers. Nothing illegal at all."

"Is there anything that might be thought of as evidence of a crime in that bag?" Tubby was wondering if this conversation might be being tape-recorded. He had recently sat through a few hours of a local judge's bribery trial, based largely on taped telephone conversations, and now he was paranoid whenever a client made any unusual suggestions. It cramped his spontaneity, since his clients were coming up with wild ideas all the time, but you had to be careful.

Darryl looked indignant. "Heck no," he protested. "You

think I'm crazy? You're a lawyer. I know you don't want any bad stuff. And by the way, I brought you the rest of your retainer. I made out the check for fifteen thousand dollars. Is that okay?" He pulled an envelope from his blazer pocket and offered it to Tubby.

Tubby got a warm feeling from Darryl. "Yes, that's fine." What the hell, he thought. "Sure, you can leave the bag here. Try to get it out this week, though. I may need to fit something into my safe that's actually related to my law practice, you understand."

"Tubby, it's not going to be a problem. I really appreciate it. Look, I got to run. Call me at the bar if you hear anything. And you know I always got a table reserved for you."

"Sure, Darryl. And think about your situation a little bit. Call me if you have something I can deal with. Say hi to Monique."

After Darryl left, Tubby picked up the bag and squeezed it with his fingers. He couldn't tell much about what was inside, but he was pretty sure it was paper. He held it up to the light but nothing showed through the fabric. He smelled it. The zipper had a tiny lock on it. Easy enough to force. Tubby shook his head at his own foolishness in accepting responsibility for anything that belonged to Darryl, but he did try to accommodate his paying clients. He opened the safe built into the cupboard below the bookshelves and stowed the bag inside next to a stack of wills. He spent a moment watching an old man and a young girl play a graceful game of tennis on the hotel roof below, then forced himself to go back to reading his vagueness exception.

So much of the law was really a drag, he thought. It took straightforward disagreements and drew them out so much that the litigants finally screamed for relief or surrender, whichever would make it all stop. As an alternative to gun battles in the street, it was pretty good, but hardly anybody ever felt like a winner and absolutely nobody appreciated the lawyers. It was easy to feel sorry for yourself in this game.

But then look at Darryl. Tubby's father had told him, whenever he got down in the dumps, to think about people with real problems. He did, and it helped.

Sometimes, to pick up a few bucks, Casey tracked down people who skipped bail. If he could catch the guy at home, he had enough authority to make the arrest and bring him before the court downtown. He collected from the bondsman for his services.

A prisoner at the jail had given Casey a tip that a minor pimp called Phil the Phoneman was staying with his mother in Algiers, the part of New Orleans across the Mississippi River. Phil had failed to appear for his trial on a charge of promoting prostitution, causing his bondsman to risk forfeiting $5,000. So there was plenty of financial incentive to find him.

It was easy. Phil even answered the door, pretty as you please, and now he was sitting in the backseat of Casey's car. Freddie was the passenger in front. To save paying the toll on the bridge, Casey decided to take the ferry back over the river. They had to wait a few minutes in a line of cars, while listening to their captive go on and on.

"This is bullshit. Oh, man," he'd say.

"This is real bullshit. Oh, man," he'd say again.

"I cannot believe this." His hands were cuffed in front of him, not too securely, but symbolic of the fact that his day was totally shot.

They were waved onto the boat and snugged in with the other cars and trucks.

"I'm getting some air," Casey said when they were parked. He opened his door, and Freddie did the same to join him.

"How about some music at least," Phil whined.

"Shit, man, you think this is a cruise boat?" Freddie asked.

"Turn on the radio for him," Casey ordered. "Who cares?"

Freddie switched on a country station and got out of the car. He caught up with Casey, who was at the rail, looking at the brown water churned up by the ferry's powerful battle with the current. There was a tanker coming downriver fast, and the ferry paused to let it pass. Black chunks, like tree trunks or railroad ties, bobbed in the big ship's wake and floated after it in pursuit. They could hear snatches of music from the tour boats loading up at Woldenberg Park in the French Quarter. Casey had a few peanuts in his pocket, and he cracked them open, tossing the shells toward the seagulls trailing the ferry. He didn't offer any to Freddie.

"This has been a very unprofitable week," he said, almost to himself. "It is hard to believe Alvarez didn't have any money with him. I thought for sure we'd find it in his truck."

"They tore that apart," Freddie said.

"Very frustrating," Casey said.

He ate another peanut.

"I guess we'll never know unless we ask Darryl," he said, and spit out a piece of shell.

Above them the captain blew the horn, signaling their approach to the dock. The pilings groaned as the boat crunched against the pier, and the two men watched the civil servants throw heavy ropes ashore to secure the vessel. They got back in the car. Phil the Phoneman was still shaking his head, but he seemed to have calmed down some.

"This some terrible music, man," he said. "Can't you find no rhythm and blues, or something with a beat?"

Casey shut off the radio and started the car.

When he had them off the ferry he parked by a fire hydrant and told Freddie to watch the prisoner.

"I need to make a phone call," he said.

There were pay phones in the ferry terminal, and the third one Casey tried had a dial tone.

"This is Casey," he said when he made the connection.

He got an earful of complaints.

"Well, he didn't have the money on him so either he was planning a rip-off or else he'd made arrangements to buy now, pay later," Casey said.

He listened some more.

"Sure I understand it's important. I'm gonna do what I can do. I'm gonna talk to the man personally. I'm optimistic he'll cooperate with me. Darryl ain't one to put up much of a fight."

After another minute Casey hung up. He was pissed.

When he got back in the car both Phil and Freddie were popping their fingers to some Motown on the radio.

"You're a real freak, Freddie," he said sourly, and Freddie straightened up.

To the prisoner he said, "Where you're going they play the music loud all night to drown out what they're doing to each other. But you already know that, don't you, Phil?"

Phil dropped his hands and sat back in the seat.

"Oooh, cold," he said.

NINE

THERE'S AN OFF-TRACK BET-
ting parlor on Bourbon Street near Canal. From the sidewalk
you can't see what's inside because the windows are tinted
dark like the sunglasses a lifeguard wears, but there's a neon
sign outside to let you know the place is alive. Inside it is
cool, clean, and green. There are little tables and chairs, a
big television screen, and race results playing electronically
on a board, like stock prices at a New York broker's office.
There is a well-stocked bar, and waitresses come to the
tables. Outside the sun burned down, but inside Tubby was
sharing a cocktail with Jason Boaz, the inventor. Both were
watching the television screen on the wall, looking at the
horses lining up at the gate. Tubby had ten dollars down
on Peach Smoothie to place and another ten dollars on Trolley Car to win. The real live action was only a couple of
miles away at the Fairgrounds.

People described Jason as lanky. He had a long, rugged
face with a neat black beard. He wore heavy black plastic

glasses that had never been in style. Today he had on a white shirt, a string tie, and baggy blue slacks, like a chemistry professor at some Midwestern college where they admire sloppiness. He was chain-smoking stiletto menthol cigarettes and partaking of Long Island Teas, a staggering combination of four white whiskeys and Coke.

The race started, and though neither man said anything they both leaned forward a bit because they had money on it. Jason had a bet on Rock 'Em, Sock 'Em. At the end, Rock 'Em, Sock 'Em took it. Peach Smoothie came in fourth, and Trolley Car retired limping. There were claps and moans, laughter and a half-hearted Bronx cheer from the other gentlemen and ladies spending money in the place.

"Attaboy," Jason yelled when his horse came in first.

"What did you have on him?" Tubby asked.

"Fifty bucks. I had a hunch and should have bet more. I could kick myself."

"Life is rough," Tubby said and crumpled his worthless tickets into the ashtray.

"See the jockey? That's Nicky Piglia's son." Tubby looked blank. "You know, Nicky Piglia. Has a po'boy shop, whatchacallit, yeah, 'Nicky's.' Out in Marrero. He serves a half and half that's, like, mammoth."

"Any relation to Roy Piglia, who got killed when Pan Am 282 crashed out in Kenner?" asked Tubby, remembering what was far and away his most lucrative case, the one that had made it possible for him to open his downtown office, start his practice with Reggie, and buy a new car. It was a bright-yellow BMW, and he gave it to his then-wife Mattie. She sold it after they got separated, and what did she do with the money?

"I don't know, maybe they're cousins. There's got to be about a million Piglias."

Another race was starting, and Tubby had a horse in this one, too. He was betting Shake and Bake to win, but the horse was stuck in Gate 4, not such a hot spot to be in.

"So Tubby, while I got your meter off, so to speak, you think it's worth me protecting my Porta-Soak and Mow?"

Tubby couldn't remember hearing about that one. "Tell me about it," he said.

"It's a neat idea. I thought we'd talked. There's a plastic water tank, like for one of those Super Soaker water guns, just bigger. And you pump that up. You strap the tank to your back. There's a tube comes out of the top with a spray nozzle, and while you mow your grass, or do anything that gets you really hot, you can give yourself a little shower or a light mist. It's adjustable."

Tubby lost his concentration on the race, which was just now beginning, and stared at Jason to see if he was serious. Jason wasn't giving anything away. He probably was. Jason's last idea had been for a shoe that circulated cold water around your feet. Ha. Ha. He had built a prototype and showed it around. He ended up assigning his patent to a Korean manufacturer for $418,000. Tubby had done the paperwork.

"Well, Jason, it sounds kind of clumsy. Why don't people just go inside and take a shower, or jump through a sprinkler? Anyway, who mows yards anymore?"

"Kids mow yards, and kids will like this. And college kids at the beach, they will like this. We make the tanks in orange, 'Day-Glo' green, crazy colors, you know, acrylics. They'll spray each other. They'll fill it with beer."

Tubby thought he could visualize that beach party. "Hell, of course you should patent it," he said.

"That's what I think."

"Get your drawings together, come by the office, and let's talk."

"Okay, why not. It might be a big payoff item."

"You got much left from the Cool Shoe?"

"Well, it's about a hundred dollars less for every hour I sit in here."

The horses came around the stretch. Shake and Bake first, then second, then third across the finish line.

"Like I said." Jason dropped his ticket into an empty coffee cup.

"Gotta run," said Tubby. "I got a lunch at Galatoire's."

"Hope you're not treating."

"No, this is a payback. Call me at work."

Tubby walked the two blocks to the restaurant. It was almost two o'clock, which was good timing for Galatoire's. There was no line.

"Good afternoon, Mr. Dubonnet," the head waiter said softly. "We will have a table in just a moment. Are you alone?"

"Mr. Chaisson is joining me," Tubby said. The dining room was narrow, and all of the tables were full. Old waiters, most of them familiar to Tubby, carried silver platters around, trailing fragrances of fish and garlic. No women servers distracted the diners.

Tubby was shown to a table against the wall beneath an ornate mirror. He ordered a gin on the rocks. His mind drifted over the things he was supposed to do that day. Then it settled for a moment on Jynx Margolis. Was there some chemistry there? It had been so long since he had dated anybody that he had forgotten how to read the signs. She was certainly appealing, in a good, clean, middle-aged fun kind of way, a nicely tanned and very fragrant kind of way. Problems did not weigh heavily on Jynx's shoulders. Marriage to her would be difficult, he imagined. She was irrepressibly self-indulgent and sort of an airhead sometimes. But who was talking marriage? Could she really find him attractive? Hard to tell with Jynx what was actually a magnetic field and what was simply her flirtatious nature. Maybe with her it didn't matter. She was a mystery to Tubby, a bit exotic. It was flattering having an exotic try to flirt with you.

Tubby was lost in thought when E. J. Chaisson came through the door. He was slight and dapper, combing his thin blond hair straight back to accentuate his large eyes and smooth, angular face, like a hungry street kid who had picked up good manners. He wore Italian suits from Rubenstein Brothers on Canal Street and always carried a cane or umbrella. Today it was a thin brown stick with an ivory handle that Tubby saw was a carved alligator, its tail curving around and gripping the wood. E.J. hung it with a flourish on the back of the empty chair between them.

"Tubby, I intended to arrive early and hold a table for you. Did you wait long?"

"Not at all. I've just ordered a drink. Join me." Tubby waved at the waiter.

"How have you been? A Sazerac, please," Chaisson told the man who appeared beside him.

"Busy, but that's what pays the bills."

"I've also been busy. I'm going into radio."

"Are you going to be explaining legal issues to the public?"

"That's certainly a good idea." His drink arrived. E.J. took a sip and nodded to show that it was agreeable. "No, I'm starting to advertise—in Vietnamese."

"You speak Vietnamese?"

"Heck no, but my yard man does. He's been working for me for a year, and one day we start to talking about what I do. He tells me, guess what, there's about twenty thousand boat people in New Orleans who he is related to, and not one of them knows an attorney."

E.J. grinned suddenly, showing his pointed white teeth, and winked. For emphasis he snapped a little bread stick from the basket the waiter put before him, stuck a scoop of fresh butter on the end, and waved it like a conductor's baton. "He's going to bring me clients. Plus interpret for them. If I take a case, he gets a piece of the action."

Tubby finished his drink. "The Bar Association won't like that." Tubby was an expert on things the Bar Association would and wouldn't like. He'd run several money-making ideas past its ethics committee, and each time had been advised to steer clear. He was sensitive because of a problem he had had over the Pan Am crash. After Tubby had signed up one of the victims, a downtown attorney had complained that Tubby was hustling clients in the hospital. Tubby had explained, in a letter to the Bar, that the referral had come quite innocently from one of the physicians treating the poor man, a plastic surgeon named Dr. Feingold. Tubby also immediately stopped his check to the doctor, even though it was just a token of friendship. He heard no more about it from the Bar, but he had heard about the check from Dr. Feingold ever since.

"The thing is, you can't split your fees with a nonlawyer. It's unethical."

"Are you sure about that?" E.J. asked.

"Oh yeah, positive. Look it up in the rules."

"We didn't have to learn that stuff to pass the bar exam when I was in law school."

The waiter returned and took their orders. The oysters were salty, and E.J. ordered his *en brochette*. Tubby chose trout *meunière amandine*.

"Look," said Tubby, "there's ways around it. Why not just call your guy a paralegal and put him on a nice salary?"

"I don't think so," E.J. said sourly. "I'm afraid his appetite is a little bigger than that. He wants to be on the incentive plan."

"Send him to law school."

"Can't do that," E.J. said between bites of bread. "Then what would he need me for?"

"Okay, try this. Suppose you set him up an advertising company. Immigrants all love to own a company. Do you agree?" E.J. nodded. "He broadcasts advertisements in Vietnamese for your law office. You pay him according to the number of calls you receive from the ads. You have a gentlemen's understanding that, down the road, if the cases pay off he gets to raise his rates."

A peppered fillet, covered with sliced almonds, appeared before Tubby. He pricked it gently with his fork, and a puff of steam escaped, with it a light smell of daybreak and high tide at the beach. E.J. inspected his skewered oysters and bacon and inhaled with pleasure.

"Ah, this looks perfect," he crooned. "So you think that would be legal?"

"I don't see why not."

"Let me give it some thought. And I'll discuss it with Nyop. As you said, every immigrant likes to own a company."

"Like your grandfather."

"Actually, my great-grandfather," E.J. said, referring to the old Frenchman who had managed to acquire so much Vieux Carré real estate that it had taken his descendants four generations to work it down to the several blocks they now owned and leased at handsome rates. Unlike Tubby, who was originally from a hamlet called Bunkie, surrounded by sugarcane and rice plantations, and who had only landed in New Orleans because his father had gotten him into Tulane, E.J. was a pillar of New Orleans society. Never mind that several of his ancestors had been hung as outlaws by the Spaniards or the Yankees, E.J. paraded with the Krewe of Proteus, when it rode, and had flattered Tubby by inviting him to join. Tubby had declined because, at the time, he was privately too hard up for cash to pay the dues.

"How's your drug-smuggling case coming?"

"Okay. How did you hear about that?"

"I saw your name in the newspaper—the story about the bail hearing."

Tubby finished chewing a bite of fish, and stabbed a crisp slice of tomato. "There's not much for me to do. He got caught with the goods."

"Did they have a tip?"

"Oh, yes, but nobody is telling where it came from. The DEA field office down there was well prepared though they're still having to explain why all they caught was Alvarez."

"I've always thought it a little distressing how criminals turn each other in all the time. Where's the honor? Wouldn't it be terrible if professionals did that to each other?"

"We're slightly more reliable, I guess, but that's changing, too."

"A toast to the reticent nature of officers of the court everywhere. What do you think Alvarez was planning to do with the pot?"

"Sell it, of course," Tubby said. "For all I know he sells it out of the back room at Champs. Do you know Darryl?"

"Sure, I've eaten and imbibed a few at Champs. But it's a total surprise to me that he's in that league. So much pot must cost a lot of money."

"The police say its street value was in the millions. They didn't catch him with any cash, though. It probably left with the boat."

"Have you been over to Champs since his arrest?"

"No, but Darryl comes to see me. He was by yesterday."

"What's going to happen to him?"

"He'll probably go to prison for a while, unless he points the finger at someone else."

"Just what I was saying. Everyone feels this need to turn someone else in. They pass around guilt like a bottle of wine."

"Not Darryl. So far he's not talking, though he's sweating a little. I guess he's more like one of your professionals."

"Well, I have always appreciated discretion."

"You ain't never been in jail, *cher*."

"And I'm the second generation of my family with that distinction," Chaisson said with obvious pride.

TEN

I T WASN'T LONG BEFORE Darryl opened up a little more to Monique about the money. She was behind the bar, mixing an old-fashioned for the nice old man who pumped gas at the marina, when this skinny kid with long blond hair, good-looking but vacant and needy somehow, sat down. He waved until she paid him some attention.

"Is Darryl Alvarez here?" he asked. He had a look of desperation.

"I don't know. If he's here, he's busy. What will you have?"

"Oh, not really anything to drink. But I need to speak to Mr. Alvarez. It's important."

"What's important about it?"

"I've got to tell him in person."

"Sorry," she said and started to move away.

"Wait a second," he pleaded. "Do you know who Tubby Dubonnet is?"

Monique recognized the name of Darryl's lawyer.

"Yeah, I do."

That brightened up the young man's face. He was making contact.

"He's my brother-in-law. And he's sent me with a message. I've got to give it personally to Darryl Alvarez."

"Okay, we'll see. What's your name?"

"Harold," said Harold.

She rang the office on the house phone. Darryl answered "Yes" the way he always did.

"I've got a guy down here named Harold who says he's Tubby Dubonnet's brother-in-law. Do you want to talk to him? He says he's got a message, and it's important, et cetera." She was watching Harold empty the peanut bowl on the bar.

"Send him up," Darryl said.

Monique told one of the girls to show Harold the way. He said thanks a lot very sincerely and pocketed a handful of matches.

Not much later she saw him come back down the stairs and go out the front door toward the street. After work, she asked Darryl what it was about. He must have had a little toot because he really started talking.

"That little fruitcake tried to score," he said. "He said he wanted some crack for Tubby. I don't know him from Adam. I would have thrown him out right then, but I heard what he had to say in case, you know, it might be for real. I didn't know if he was trying to set me up or what. Finally I told the asshole I'd have to call Tubby to check him out, and he started talking a mile a minute, trying to run a con on me. He gave me all these reasons why I couldn't call

Tubby. It was just bullshit. Finally I had enough and told him to get the fuck out of here."

"Is he really related to your lawyer?"

"I seriously doubt it. This guy is a real putz."

"Do you think Mr. Dubonnet is into drugs?"

"I'd have to doubt that, too. I don't think that would be his type of action. Horses, maybe. Not drugs."

"Why? You got the idea lawyers don't do cocaine?"

"I wouldn't make that mistake. Lawyers are the worst. Hey, my biggest headaches come from lawyers. Lawyers and cops."

"Cops like Casey?" she asked. It slipped out.

"How do you know his name?"

"He told me the night, you know, that you introduced me to him." She was freaking, but he didn't see it.

"Casey's no cop," he said. "He's some kind of investigator for Sheriff Mulé. He's just a hood, really. He runs little scams down at the jail and does whatever the sheriff tells him to do. He wasn't involved in this deal. I wonder more about the guy who was with Casey, the one who actually brought me the money." Darryl didn't tell her the man's name.

"Are you thinking he set you up?"

"Maybe, but I don't see how. He didn't know the when or the where. I made the arrangements myself, with people I've done business with in the past. The guy you saw introduced me to the major player, the son of a bitch who financed this fucking disaster here. This guy's very rich. He's got a big house in the Garden District, with the slave quarters and everything. I've been down by it. I've never been inside, of course. He wouldn't want the little lady to see me. He acts like a Greek god or something. He knows people who want to put up some money. High risk. High yield. All cash. Can I provide the product? Will I pick it up and distribute it? Of course I will. Then everybody makes lots of money. Their investment pays off well. He's the guy I felt I could trust, 'cause he's so rich. But I don't know. He's just not my type. That may be where I got in trouble. Maybe I misread him."

Monique didn't say anything.

"That's why I had you hold the money, Monique. Just because I wasn't sure."

"What's he going to do now?"

"I know he wants to talk to me real bad, just like I want to talk to him. We need to straighten out what happened. I need to find out what he's going to do for me. Right now I'd guess he's pretty anxious to get his money back. I just haven't thought of a safe way for us to get together yet."

"Do you think he can get you out of this?"

"I think he can. He knows the right strings to pull. The question is will he pull them. I'll say this. If he doesn't get me out of this jam, he's going to be short one big pile of money."

Darryl didn't tell Monique what Tubby had said about the eight years. After he wound down a little bit, they made gentle love on the upholstered chair in the office, with the television blaring and the wall monitors flashing live scenes from the barroom below. Later, Darryl sat in front of the TV, flipping channels. Monique curled up on the chair for a little nap, and before she fell asleep she prayed that Darryl would never find out what she had done.

* * *

On Mondays, Champs was closed until late in the after-noon to permit a crew to come in and clean the place and give it some air. They usually finished at around noon, and the doors opened to the public at four o'clock. Darryl was there all day. Monique did some laundry in the morning and then came over on her bicycle to keep him company.

They were sitting at the empty bar, listening to a Neville Brothers tape on the sound system while they talked about this and that and watched the boats out on the lake. Darryl asked her to go upstairs and get the cash register keys. She was in the office when she heard a loud crash. Her eyes jumped to the console that monitored the downstairs area, and she saw two men, one tall and one short and broad, advancing through the front door they had just smashed open. They had some kind of guns in their hands. Her eyes went to the other monitor. Darryl had noticed something. He was standing up and reaching under the counter.

Before the men had even located Darryl, she saw him grab for the Baretta 9 he kept beneath the register. The short man saw him move and opened fire, shattering glass all over the place and catching Darryl right in the chest. He coughed, coughed, and coughed and went down hard on his back. Both men ran over to the bar, and the short one kicked Darryl. The big guy was pissed off. He grabbed the short man and stuck a gun in his face. He said something, then pushed him away in disgust. He looked up at the camera, and Monique recognized Casey. The two men looked at each other, and then moved off camera in the direction of the stairs.

She thought about barricading herself in the office and calling the police, but to her Casey was the police. She got out of there and ran down the hall. She could hear them coming at her up the stairs. She slipped through the lounge as quickly and quietly as she could and opened the French doors to the balcony. She closed them behind her and crouched in a corner by the railing. If they came that way, she planned to jump into the lake.

She heard the sound of wood splintering. That would be the office door. There were more thuds and sounds of things being thrown around. It seemed to go on for a long time, but maybe it was just a few minutes. Then she heard heavy footsteps running down the stairs. Five minutes later, she pushed the doors open slowly and tiptoed across the floor. It was all quiet below, and she slipped downstairs softly. The bar was a mess. The front door was broken open. There was busted glass everywhere. She ran over to Darryl, and there was just lots wrong with him. Blood was pumping out of his chest, and there were large red holes in his shirt and big pieces of flesh hanging off and his eyes were wide open and crossed and his tongue was sticking out of his mouth. He looked horrified. She was horrified. She tried to push his chest back together but it wouldn't go, and she cried.

A young couple, thinking they might each have a Corona and lime on a pretty afternoon, came in and found them like that. After they got over the surprise, they called the police.

ELEVEN

TUBBY LIKED TO HAVE A small breakfast at a coffee shop on Maple Street uptown called PJ's. Back when he was married, Mattie made a big morning meal for the whole family. The divorce had ended that, of course, and for some strange reason it also seemed to have robbed him of his morning appetite. He did enjoy being served, however. He stopped uptown because it was a quiet oasis on his way to the office. One of the nice things about PJ's was that he hardly ever saw anyone he knew, except the congregation of regulars who were starting to recognize him and would sometimes nod.

The array of blends and flavors was confusing to him. Tubby was not much on variety in his coffee. He tried hazelnut once, and it put him in a bad mood, so he stuck with what they called "French roast with chicory." Sometimes a muffin, sometimes not.

This morning he was trying a banana pecan muffin while reading the newspaper. He sat on the outdoor patio, which was separated from the street by a low fence. His attention wandered to a black guy wearing jeans and a basketball jersey, leaning against the rail with a quarter stuck in his ear. Tubby wondered if that were functional, like the man was ready to use a pay phone, or purely ornamental. Must be a fad, he decided, better than a penny in the loafers but cheaper than gold stars on the teeth. The breeze from the river nearby blended with the smell of coffee roasting and carried with it the familiar jarring sounds of freight trains coupling by the levee.

He finished the front section of the *Times-Picayune* and picked up the metro news. On the first page, in the bottom right-hand corner, the headline read: TAVERN OWNER SHOT: POLICE SEEK KILLERS. He read the story quickly:

Police are seeking leads to the identity of two men seen leaving the scene of Monday afternoon's fatal shooting at Champs, a popular lakefront bar. According to a witness, two white males, both described as being in their late thirties or forties, entered the establishment on Sunset Boulevard before it opened for the evening and shot manager Darryl Alvarez to death. Police report that he was shot four times, three times in the chest and once in the face, after an apparent struggle. The motive, police say, may have been robbery. Two men were seen leaving the restaurant shortly before four o'clock p.m. by a woman arriving for work. According to a man delivering pizza in the area, they reportedly drove away in a dark red or maroon car with Louisiana license plates. Mr. Alvarez was under indictment in Federal Court in New Orleans, stemming from his arrest for marijuana smuggling in July. When arrested near Caillou Lake in Terrebonne Parish he was allegedly loading 15 bales of marijuana, with an estimated street value of $3 million, into a truck. Mr. Alvarez has no known survivors.

Tubby sped downtown on Freret Street, going too fast past school children in uniforms, jumping rope at the bus stops, and vegetable vendors setting up their stands by the curbs. The day was already hot, but he had not taken the time to put up the top on the convertible. He navigated the spiral-up ramp of the parking garage in dangerous time. While riding up in the elevator, he hummed and stroked the nonexistent beard on his face.

Cherrylynn had not yet arrived. Tubby went quickly into his office and went straight to the safe. He knelt down and opened it. Yes, the gym bag was there. He pulled it out and carried it to his desk. Fishing around in the top drawer, he found a staple remover and used it to grip the little lock. Then he stuck a letter opener through the hasp and twisted it hard. The lock bent and popped, and he unzipped the bag.

He wasn't surprised that it contained money, but the eye-appealing fact was that it contained lots of money. Tubby forgot to breathe for a minute, then he moved fast.

The bills were already sorted and separated into stacks. Most were wrinkled $100s, but some were $20s or $50s. Tubby pulled them out and did a quick count on his desk. It was impossible to be completely accurate, but it looked like about a million dollars. He stuffed everything back into the bag and was zipping it back up when Cherrylynn walked in.

"Oh, I didn't know you were in yet, Mr. Dubonnet. I thought I heard somebody back here." She was obviously interested in the bag.

"I just got an early start today," he said.

"Did you see Darryl Alvarez was murdered?" she asked from the doorway, then started to walk in.

"No, I didn't. That's terrible. How shocking."

"It happened at his bar . . ."

"Could you please fix me a cup of coffee, black." Except when he was schmoozing with clients, he had not asked her to fix him a cup of coffee in the last three years, so she looked surprised. It stopped her, though.

"Why sure, boss. Coming up."

She went out and pulled the door behind her. She gave him a last looking-over before the door closed. Always curious.

Clutching the gym bag, Tubby went to the door. Cherrylynn was not in the front reception area but was in the kitchen, so the path to the outside door of the office was clear. Tubby reached it in two steps. As he went out he yelled, "Forget the coffee, Cherrylynn. I need to go out for a few minutes."

The elevator came, and no one was inside. Tubby stripped off his suit jacket and draped it over the bag. It certainly did not conceal that he was holding something, but maybe it disguised what it was. He went back to his car the way he had come. He drove, considerably slower, with the bag beside him on the passenger seat, thinking deep thoughts.

He tried to concentrate enough to analyze his various duties. First, if this money was evidence, he was supposed to turn it over to the police. There was an ethical rule on point, he was sure. Something about not engaging in conduct prejudicial to the administration of justice. He didn't recall the details, but he thought that was the gist of it. What an obscure and misty proposition that was! He was also sworn to maintain the confidences of his clients. In this case his client was dead, a complicating factor. But did he have no responsibility to his client's memory? Was there a duty there? It was all complex.

Anyhow, maybe it was not dirty money, just some dough Darryl had squirreled away. Maybe Darryl had won it at the track, or making book on football. If the police got hold of it, it would be gone forever. They would protect and serve themselves. Darryl had no heirs that Tubby knew about. It was doubtful Darryl was safeguarding it for someone else, because who would trust him with that much money? The best thing, Tubby figured, was to hold on to it and see what happened. It would be smartest to hide it at his house. He couldn't think of anyplace else. Tubby headed up St. Charles Avenue.

He pulled into his driveway and parked behind the boat he stored in the carport beside his garage. Before the engine shut off he hit the automatic door opener perched on his dash. Tubby took the money into the garage, which he used for a workshop, and buzzed the door closed. He cleared a space on his workbench and dumped the money out. A careful count showed that it totaled $950,000, a little less than he had thought at first, but no problem. The bills were old and weathered and looked right at home among his hammers and hand saws. They smelled good in here, with the linseed oil and wood shavings. He thought about the bag. Should he lose it? Well, maybe it might turn out to be evidence, too. Probably better to keep it for the time being as well. Tubby packed the loot back in the bag and carried it all outside. He was starting to sweat.

His boat, stored outside, was not an impressive craft, but a weather-beaten twenty-footer with an inboard motor that he used for pulling the girls waterskiing. He also occasionally took it out with Raisin Partlow, one of the few friends he had who still enjoyed fishing and beer. He climbed on board and rummaged around through a bunch of tangled crab traps. There was a compartment for tackle that was now empty. Neighborhood kids, or more likely his former brother-in-law Harold, had cleaned him out of tools and gear a couple of times, and now he did not keep anything of value around the boat. There was a storage area in the bow, stuffed full of some moldy life jackets. Tubby pushed the gym bag among them and covered it up. For some reason he did not want to have the money in his house, and he thought probably all the local thieves had given up on the boat by now. This was considered a good neighborhood. Lots of trees and lawyers, close to the universities, but if you left a bicycle in the yard unguarded for more than half an hour it would be gone. The neighborhood hired an off-duty policeman to drive around at night. He was a cheerful guy. He had never caught anyone that Tubby knew about, but he'd once helped Tubby push his car down the street when the battery died, so Tubby never complained about chipping in his monthly dues.

Tubby stuffed his shirttails back into his pants and looked

around. Only one of his neighbors was visible—a silver-haired lady in a flowery housedress, watering her plants under the sprawling shade of a live oak tree down the block. She was not paying him any attention. Across the street, an upstairs window curtain seemed to move, but he could not really be sure. You never could tell for certain in this neighborhood, with all the trees for cover and the houses close together, who was seeing what. It was generally a good bet that someone was looking around, as nervous as everybody permanently stayed about burglaries and other forms of mischief.

Tubby tried to look normal, though he knew he could not quite make it since he was wearing a tie and stumbling around in a parked boat in the middle of the day. Oh well. He disembarked, dusted off his hands theatrically, and hitched up his pants. He got into his car and backed it out of the driveway. As he drove downtown he passed gaily dressed groups of tourists waiting for the streetcar at every other block. They were lighthearted. He was not.

TWELVE

TUBBY SPENT THE REST OF the day in his office. He even sent Cherrylynn out for a roast beef sandwich with extra gravy from Ditcharo's down the street. Mainly he tried to read and write various things requiring concentration, and to stay off the phone in case anybody he wanted to talk to called. Cherrylynn announced several times that people he did not want to talk to were on the phone, but each time he told her to take a message.

He went home early and avoided his boat. He heated up a bowl of his housekeeper's leftover gumbo for supper and ate it in front of the TV, watching an old Errol Flynn movie. The phone rang once, and his answering machine caught it. Nobody left a message. He gave up and went to bed early, but he had a hard time getting to sleep. He tried to erase all negative thoughts, any thoughts, but it didn't work. Finally he got up and had a couple of shots of gin, and that did the trick.

The next morning was more of the same. He moved

around on automatic pilot, but his mind raced. He knew that outside there was more cash than he could ever use, but somewhere another shoe was about to drop. There was a good chance it was aiming for him. When he was a kid he had gotten caught stealing a pen from a card shop, and the owner had called his mother. She sat him down on the bed and asked him why he had done it. Didn't he have enough pens at home? Since then he had never wanted to do anything that could ever make him feel so guilty. Still, he was no asshole, and only an asshole gives up almost a million bucks before he is pretty sure he has to. The thing to do was to go about his business and pretend it never happened. Tubby did not like moral dilemmas. He tried to avoid them whenever possible and to see things in practical terms—what worked and what didn't. This monster had fangs, though, and a good bite on him.

He skipped breakfast at PJ's and ate toast. Then he dressed and drove down to Broad Street, site of the imposing Criminal Courts building. Its New Deal architecture dominated an area of vacant lots, boarded-up businesses, jails, and storefronts for bail bondsmen. There was a crowd of mostly black people waiting for buses on the corner, and another squatting on the courthouse steps munching Popeye's and drinking Cokes while waiting for the system to grind along until it was their turn. It was easy to spot the lawyers hustling across the street and trotting up the steps since they wore suits and didn't look scared. Next door was the ancient Parish Prison where guards were posted above the sidewalk in concrete turrets like miniature lighthouses, connected to each other by strands of razor wire. Visitors queued up at one gate, waiting to be searched so they could go in and talk about money, and kids dropping out of school, and court dates being postponed, with whichever poor fucked-up loved ones of theirs had the misfortune to be locked inside. They looked like they had spent all their lives in this line or one just like it. Besides the helpless, why was it that nobody but cranks, crooks, and characters hung out around the halls of justice? It was not even nine o'clock and it was already hot.

Above twenty granite steps, towering brass-clad doors opened onto a cavernous hallway, wide and tall as a cathedral. It was cool and quiet there. Footsteps echoed off the walls, and the small knots of people congregating outside the courtroom doors spoke furtively. Other doors along the hallway were always shut, hiding places Tubby had never been.

The courthouse crowd—the judges, magistrates, clerks, cops, secretaries, and jailers—used to be all white. Today the faces were nearly all black. It was something you noticed, no big deal. The quality of justice wasn't much different as far as he could tell, though some of the new judges were more idealistic than their predecessors. Trouble was, the volume of business was so great that there was precious little time for fairness, compassion, mercy, all those good things. Tubby had been into most of the judges' chambers and courtrooms here, and he could pass back and forth through the bars of the sheriff's jail. He was part of the in-crowd, not like the folks outside on the steps, but the place still gave him the shivers, every time.

Inside Courtroom L he saw Sandy Shandell, his medical malpractice client, sitting quiet and erect on one of the long mahogany benches, a sinner in church. Sandy turned around when the door opened and waved when he recognized Tubby, giving him a big smile. Not content with one legal problem—his spotted skin—Sandy had also been busted for assaulting a policeman. He had somehow raised his own bail and was now due to be arraigned. Tubby could have instructed him on the telephone how to enter a plea of not guilty all by himself, but Sandy had a volatile personality, to say the least, which seemed to produce an immediate allergic reaction in law enforcement personnel, so Tubby came down.

Sandy was at his theatrical best. He was wearing a silky bright-yellow blouse with horizontal black stripes, and burgundy slacks with vertical white stripes. Thus he made your eyes cross even if you just glanced at him. He also had a purple scarf wrapped around his neck and thrown back over his shoulder. Tubby knew he was sensitive about his appearance since Dr. Feingold's treatments. Where it was visible, on his cheeks and hands, you could tell there were pronounced chocolate drops on his otherwise cream-colored skin. His case, Tubby knew, would be worth substantially more if Sandy were a pretty young Sophie Newcomb grad instead of a flamboyant French Quarter cross-dresser. A jury might wonder why a few dozen liver spots would matter to someone like Sandy, but Tubby knew how vain she was. Depending on the context, Tubby sometimes envisioned Sandy as a he, and sometimes as a she. He had quit fighting it, and now used whatever pronoun came out naturally at the time.

"Hey, Sandy, where y'at?" Tubby squeezed in next to him.

"Tubby, thanks for coming," Sandy gasped. That fruity

touch was one of his mannerisms, which he sometimes turned off. He launched into his story.

"This was absolutely not my fault. I was smoking a cigarette—I could use one now—outside of Major Cee's on Bourbon Street, when this asshole cop, I think his name is Matthews, comes up and asks me what kind of pistol I'm packing. That's right. I thought he meant a gun. I said, 'What on Earth do you mean?' and he taps my crotch with that plastic club they all carry and says, 'Have you made your trip to Sweden yet for your operation?' "

"You're kidding."

"No! And you know how sensitive I am about that. And I don't like anybody, especially some cretin cop from Arabi, touching my genitalia without an invitation."

"So what did you do?"

"I called him a stupid honky yat motherfucking pig. Tubby, I know I shouldn't have done that, but I was really mad. And then as soon as I said it I was scared, and I knew I was in trouble."

"What did he do?" Tubby caught sight of Sandy's ring, a cameo. It was an ivory profile of a woman, her hair braided above her forehead, on a faint pink field. Was it something Sandy's mother might have given him, or was it one of those pieces of other people's history that you bought in a flea market or the antique shops that lined Chartres Street? Tubby didn't know a lot about Sandy's private affairs, thank God. He had heard, however, that Sandy had a significant other who was HIV positive. Sandy's life was not all peaches and cream.

"He said, 'Get in the car,' just like that, and arrested me. I said to myself, 'Sandy, the man's an asshole. He is not tuned in to reality. Just do as he says.' I have a little voice that sometimes gets me out of these things."

"He didn't hit you or anything?"

"No."

"That's good."

"I think they're afraid to start a fight with me. I think they're worried I might bite them or something and give them AIDS. Even when he put the handcuffs on me, he tried not to actually let his fingers touch me."

"All right. Did anybody see this?"

"Sure, lots of people, but I don't know who most of them are. Miss Nancy was there and saw it."

That didn't help much. Miss Nancy was a gray-haired street lady in the French Quarter, who cast spells on the people she passed on the sidewalk.

"Listen, Sandy. This is no big deal. The cop may not even show up for trial, and anyway it's just going to be a fine. Have you got any money now?"

"Only about fifty dollars."

"Well, you pay that to me, and we'll just plead you not guilty. Save your pennies. This may not come up again for six months, and then you can decide whether to pay or fight it."

"Whatever you say, Tubby. What happens now?"

"I'll be right back." Tubby went up to the clerk in front, and told him that his client, Sandy Shandell, was in court and wished to plead not guilty to a charge of assaulting a police officer. The clerk called out Sandy's name, just to be sure he was there, took a long look at him, and shook his head at Tubby. That was that. Trial date in October.

Tubby turned aside to let the lawyer who was pushing in

from behind have some room and saw the bailiff waving him over. "Hi, Janelle," he said to the black officer leaning against the jury rail.

"Good morning, Tubby. I've been keeping an eye out for you. Sheriff Mulé wants to see you."

"Me, what the heck for?"

"Couldn't tell you. He saw your name on today's docket and said ask you to drop by if I saw you."

Tubby had no idea what that was about. He contributed nothing to the sheriff at election time. They shook hands when their paths crossed at testimonial dinners and such, which was not often, but he had never actually had a meeting with the great Mulé. Tubby went back to where Sandy was sitting and told him to go stand in line at the rear of the courtroom and wait till his name was called. They would give him a notice telling him to come back for trial in October. It would take about an hour, and Tubby would see him later.

"And let me collect the fifty dollars for today, as long as you've got it with you."

"Sure, Tubby, but I've got to take a cab home."

"Well, make it forty-five."

Sandy pulled crisp bills from her purse, and Tubby accepted them with dignity.

"All square," he said.

Sheriff Mulé's office was in the Community Correctional Center across the street. The heat smacked you as soon as you emerged into the sunlight, radiating off the white concrete of the jail. One of the nondescript buildings across the way had been painted over with a mural tracing the signal events in American history—the Revolutionary War, the

Indian Wars, the Civil War, the World Wars, and Vietnam. It was signed "Sheriff Mulé's Art in Prison Program," but in truth it had been started by Mulé's much admired predecessor, a Mediterranean lawman who, in New Orleans fashion, had retired to run an Irish pub in the French market. Looking at the painting, Tubby reflected that nobody ever seemed to remember Korea.

Beneath the exploding cannon shot, screaming eagles, and painted flags was a praline lady sitting on a metal folding chair. She wore a red bandana on her black head in the traditional way, and had on a double-breasted pink raincoat pulled tight around her despite the temperature. Her wares were on a cardboard boxtop on her lap. Tubby crossed the street to admire the round candies she had arranged neatly on a sheet of wax paper.

"How much are they?" he asked.

"Yes, sir, one dollar," she said. "And they're the best in town. Just take your pick."

Tubby studied his choices. "How's business?" he asked.

"Business isn't never much good. I'm getting whooped by them vending machines inside."

"Why don't you move up by the bus stop?"

"They run me off up there. Or them kids try to steal whatever little I got. Down here they leave me alone. Besides, I got a godson in there." She pointed across the street. "I think maybe he can see me."

"Your godson's in jail?" Tubby picked out the one he wanted.

"Yes, I'm sorry to say it." She handed Tubby a caramel-colored praline, thick with pecan halves coated with sugar melted in cream and vanilla.

"How long has he been in?"

"Oh, I'd say better than a year."

"And he's still here? I didn't think they stayed that long in the jail. Maybe he's been sent to one of the prisons."

"I couldn't say. That's where he went in, though, and he hasn't come out."

Tubby bit his praline. A piece cracked off and Tubby grabbed at it and missed. He sadly watched it hit the sidewalk.

"What's your godson's name?" he asked.

"Jerome, Jerome Cook," she said.

"Well, I hope he gets out soon."

"I sure hope so, too," she said.

Tubby nodded to her and walked back across the street. Going up the wide steps to the Correctional Center he passed a group of guards standing around eating candy bars together. Their black uniforms made him nervous. They herded, washed, fed, and processed the five thousand or so prisoners, more than most countries confined, which Orleans Parish held on a daily basis, rode in Mardi Gras parades on horseback, and campaigned for Sheriff Mulé every four years. The sheriff reigned over them, dozens of public buildings, tent cities full of inmates, and millions of dollars. Mulé was a man to be reckoned with.

The guard at the front desk told Tubby to have a seat, which he was glad to do until the perspiration chilled off his forehead. After a minute he got up and went back to the desk.

"I need to see if you've got a man in here," he told the guard.

"What's his name?"

"Jerome Cook."

"Okay, let's see." The guard tapped information into his computer console, whistling tunelessly between his teeth.

"Jerome Rasheed Cook," he said. "Yep, we got him."

"What's he charged with?" Tubby asked.

Clickety-click, the man's fingers moved over the keys.

"That's funny. I can't exactly tell you. It doesn't seem to be on the screen."

"How long has he been in here?"

"I don't know that either. This doesn't show any information on him." He looked up at Tubby and shrugged his shoulders. "I don't know what the problem is."

"Can you deliver something to him?"

"You're a lawyer, right?"

"Yeah."

"What do you want to leave for him?"

"Just give him my card." Tubby reached into his coat for his wallet and slipped out his white business card. The guard took it.

"Will you see that he gets this?"

"Sure," said the guard. "There'll be someone going up to the cells in a few minutes. I'll have them carry it up."

"Thanks," Tubby said and sat back down. After a few more minutes, the guard's phone rang and his name was called. The guard pointed him toward the elevator that led to the sheriff's executive offices above. A quick ride later he was greeted by an attractive woman with a pile of curly blond hair, also in a black uniform, who took him through the door to the sheriff's splendid office. You could hold court in here, Tubby thought. The city skyline could be admired through its picture windows. The floor was thickly carpeted, and the walls were covered with hunting trophies—cats, big birds, a bear's head, even a stuffed alligator. Mulé, a small man, peeked above his desk twenty paces from the door. He was almost hidden behind an enormous stuffed bird of prey.

Mulé stood up and extended his hand when Tubby came in. He was wearing a suit, brown as mud, with wide lapels.

"Howya doing, Tubby? Thanks for coming by."

"Sure, Sheriff. You could have just picked up the phone."

"No, I wanted to have a face-to-face, and I heard you were coming down today."

"You've really got your antennae up."

"I try to take care of my friends. It ain't always easy. Would you like some coffee?"

"Sure, thanks."

Mulé pushed a button on his telephone and an inmate cautiously opened the door.

"For this man, coffee, Pedro."

Tubby told him to make it black, and Pedro disappeared.

"I see where Darryl Alvarez got shot," Mulé said.

"That's right."

"Did he ever say who his business associates were?"

"Not to me. What's your interest in this, Sheriff?"

"My interest is in keeping drugs off the streets. Also, he was one of my campaign supporters. I hate to see any of my supporters go like that."

"Yeah. It's a shame. He had a lot of friends."

"I know you were one of them."

"Not really. I got the case through Reggie Turntide, my partner. He doesn't do criminal work."

"That's right," the sheriff beamed. "Darryl hadn't made his deal with the U.S. Attorney, had he?"

"No. You could ask the U.S. Attorney the same thing."

"My relations with the man aren't that good," the sheriff said with a grimace. That sounded right. A couple of weeks before the *Times-Picayune* had leaked the news that a federal grand jury was investigating various allegations of unconstitutional behavior at the jail.

"Any idea who he was working for?"

"Hell no, Sheriff, and I don't even speculate. The last thing I want is to be hauled before some grand jury investigating organized crime."

"Right. That's just the way it should be."

The sheriff stood up and circled his desk. He put his hand on Tubby's shoulder and gave it a squeeze, almost as if he wanted to pick him out of the chair.

"Thanks for coming by, Tubby. I really appreciate your help."

Tubby, rising, said, "I don't know what help I gave you."

"You satisfied my curiosity. At least part of it."

Mulé showed Tubby the door. Exiting, Tubby almost collided with Pedro returning with a Styrofoam cup of coffee on a tray. "I had to make it fresh, sir," he said.

"That's okay. Maybe the sheriff would like it."

"No, sir. He don't drink nothing but Kool-Aid."

That was baloney, Tubby knew. Sheriff Mulé had twice hit the papers for being drunk and highly disorderly in very odd unsherifflike places, but he had yet to get locked up in his own jail.

Tubby smiled again at the receptionist with the big hair, thinking that the black uniforms certainly looked sexier on the women than the men, and he got the elevator back to the ground floor. It was a relief to step out the front door into the free world. Mulé had showed an awful lot of interest in one crooked bartender. He did not like any part of his conversation with the sheriff. The man was connected—to the good guys and also to some characters too shadowy to classify. He had goons working for him who beat on prisoners, or so it was rumored. Maybe all jailers did. But there was also a newspaper reporter who had written about sex and drug rackets in the jail and who had been mugged so badly that he lost sight in one eye, culprits unknown. He had left town for a safer assignment. There was the uppity jailhouse lawyer who had filed dozens of suits over conditions at the jail, who was found with his throat slashed in the shower, done in, said the authorities, by his fellow inmates. All this was smoke, rumors, or allegations the sheriff had defeated in lawsuits. On the flip side was the celebrated community service—no charity gala was complete without him—but still it made you think.

Tubby figured he needed to do something about the money soon. He was coming to the conclusion that there was something he wanted and something he did not want. He did not want the gym bag to be in his boat much longer. He did want the money.

A once-pretty redhead on the downside of thirty shook her fanny, cellulite and all, in the face of an old Cuban stuffing an ashtray full of cigarettes in one of the seedy strip joints that had survived on upper Decatur Street. A couple of cop types Ali knew were at a tiny round table in the dark, leaning against the wall, having a private conversation. The taller of the two, a man they called Casey, waved Ali over.

"You used to have a girl named Monique work here?" he asked.

"We get lots of girls. About when would that be?"

"About a year ago. You know who I'm talking about."

"Not really."

"Brown hair, healthy-looking, real country, all-American type. I'm sure she was real popular."

"Okay, yeah. I might remember her."

"You probably fucked her," said the short fat guy with Casey. He was called Freddie, and he always had a radio or a pair of handcuffs hanging off his belt to show he was in law enforcement. Freddie burped up Budweiser.

Ali didn't say anything.

"She turned tricks with the customers, didn't she?" Casey asked.

Ali shrugged.

"When's the last time you saw her?"

"If we're talking about the same girl, not since she quit."

"You wouldn't be fooling me now, would you, Ali? She wouldn't have come by and given you something to keep for her, would she?"

"No."

"This is a big investigation. It's not just me asking, it's the Sheriff."

Ali didn't know if that was bullshit or not. These half-assed policemen always talked like that, but Sheriff Mulé had once been in the joint in Casey's company, so it was a possibility. Mulé had tipped well. It didn't matter either way to Ali. He didn't give a rat's ass for Sheriff Mulé and the answer was the same anyway.

"She didn't leave me nothing."

Casey turned to look at Freddie, and Ali walked away. They might not be finished talking, but he was. He moved softly around the dingy room, emptying ashtrays, guiding his bulk by memory and night radar.

"She's got to have hidden it somewhere at Champs," Freddie told Casey. "She don't go nowhere else."

"That's real smart, Freddie. Of course, we would have had the money by now if you weren't such an incredibly dumb fuck."

"Hey, he had a gun. What was I supposed to do?"

"Not cut his head off, asshole. They can't talk that way."

"I didn't know that fucking gun would shoot like that. We didn't have anything that would fire so fast when I was growing up."

"You should have told me if you didn't know what you were doing, Freddie. I could have got you a .45 or something."

"If we was to do it now, I'd do it right. I'd have it set on single shot."

"Let's roll back the camera and you can do it right this time."

"We all make mistakes, Casey."

"Gimme a break, Freddie. We're supposed to be professionals. You can't hold yourself up as a professional and say things like 'We all make mistakes.' "

Freddie looked glum.

"We all make mistakes," mimicked Casey. "For Christ's sake, let's get out of here."

"I really am sorry."

Casey put his hand on Freddie's wrist. "I forgive you. Everybody forgives you. Just concentrate a little more in the future."

Freddie said he would do that.

After they left, Ali called Monique on the phone. He told her about Casey's and Freddie's visit and the parts of their conversation he had overheard.

"Those are the same fucks who killed Darryl," she said.

Tubby crossed over the Interstate on the Broad Street overpass and drove back to his house. The route took him past the Wembley tie plant, which always reminded him to check his own for gravy spots. Damn! What a stupid place to wear a fifty-dollar piece of silk. He parked and climbed into the boat. The bag was where he had left it. That was a small surprise considering it was in an unlocked compartment on a boat sitting outdoors in a quasi-major American city. Tubby had been half hoping it would be gone and he would be relieved of the responsibility of deciding what to do with it. Maybe, he thought, the fact that the money was still there was an omen he should keep it.

After checking to see that the bag was still full, he counted out some of the cash and stuck it in his pocket. He zipped the bag up and tossed it in the trunk of his car. The day was going from extremely hot to extremely hot and muggy, so he switched on the air-conditioning as high as it would go. Then he drove to a bank branch in his neighbor-hood. Inside, after waiting a minute for another customer to conclude her business, he presented himself to a young woman seated at a desk whose name was Miss Bates, Assistant Manager, according to her plastic nameplate.

"I'd like to open an account," he told her.

"Do you already have one with us?" She smiled.

Tubby said he did not, though he had always meant to have one.

"How much do you plan to open it for?" she asked.

"One hundred thousand dollars," Tubby said. He had formed a plan to open accounts of this size at every bank in town.

"Oh my, my," Miss Bates exclaimed. "You realize, of course, that it may take a week to ten days before your funds are available to write checks on, depending on where the bank your check is drawn on is located."

"I plan to deposit cash."

Miss Bates looked disturbed. "There's a form we need you to fill out in that case. We have to report to the IRS any cash transactions over ten thousand dollars." She rustled around in her desk. "I'm sorry. I'll have to get one in the back. I won't be a minute. You can be filling out the account agreement."

Tubby was on the street in seconds, mopping sweat from behind his ears with his handkerchief, an uncomfortable bulge still in his pocket. He wished he had a female confidante. They were much better at this kind of thing than he was.

From a pay phone outside a Burger King, Tubby called

his friend, Jerry Molideau, a financial advisor whose talent was to impress well-heeled businessmen and help them shield their valuable assets from creditors, the tax man, and spouses. He sent business to Tubby, and vice versa.

He got past the secretary, and Jerry came on the line. They said hello.

"A guy just asked me a question, Jerry. I don't want to look dumb, so I thought I'd better call someone who knows the answer."

"Okay, shoot."

"My guy's got a couple of hundred thousand dollars, and he wants to put it where no one can find it. Any advice?"

"Sure. Open a Chinese restaurant and put all your cash receipts in your pocket. But seriously, that's an interesting question, and I'd be glad to talk it over in person. On the telephone my best suggestions are to bury it in a tin can in his backyard, or buy Krugerrands and stick them in a safe-deposit box."

"Have you ever heard of a rule where you have to report big cash transactions to the IRS?"

"Sure. If he buys his Krugerrands from a legitimate dealer, the dealer has to report all cash sales above ten thousand dollars to the government, just like a bank."

"Do dealers actually do that?"

"Most do. Your average jeweler or boat salesman is marginally more afraid of the IRS than he is of losing a customer."

"Sounds un-American."

"Big brother is here, Tubby." Tubby said he might drop by to discuss this further and hung up. What to do, what to do? The problem was not paying taxes on the money. It was that he could not think how he could explain to the IRS, or anybody else who might ask him, where he got $950,000.

It suddenly struck Tubby that a great many desirable things cost less than $10,000. If he wandered through downtown, where he had frequented the same shops for years, dropping wads of cash, his visits would definitely be long remembered. He had a reputation for being tight with a dollar. There were all sorts of shopping malls in the suburbs, however, and today would be just ideal to visit them.

Driving west on the Interstate he checked in with Cherrylynn on the car phone. All of his messages were routine but one. His ex-wife had called, but he would deal with her later. He told Cherrylynn he was feeling a little down in the dumps and thought he might spend the rest of the day at the track. She could take the afternoon off, he said. She was too stunned to object. After he hung up, he realized how out of character he was acting. Well, that's what financial freedom is all about. Destination Esplanade Mall. That was someplace he had never been.

Several hectic hours later he was sitting in a bistro on Veterans Boulevard called Hooters, being waited on by Hooter Girls. He was on his fourth margarita, letting the good feelings build. In the trunk of his car, besides a bag full of money, were wrapped packages containing three diamond bracelets, which Tubby planned to give to his daughters, some incredible lingerie, for a person unknown but coincidentally of a size he imagined would fit Jynx Margolis, four sports jackets for himself, some nice shoes, a pile of hardcovers he wanted to read, and a pair of tickets for a Caribbean cruise.

He had even popped into Andrea's on impulse and had a wonderful plate of crawfish ravioli and a glass of red Beneventum that cost almost as much as the food. Reinvigorated, he cruised Veterans, looking for just the right thing. And there it was. The Harley-Davidson he ordered would take about a month to come in, but it was more bike than any man could tame. He had managed to get rid of only about $48,000, which was a little disappointing, but he felt great. It was exhilarating, not so much spending the money, but suspending the moral judgment he had carried with him since his North Louisiana Sunday School teachers, not to mention his parents, got through with him. It had followed him through law school and was at the guilty heart of the majestic law he had bound himself to. Now, on a pretty day, it had lifted off his shoulders like a helium balloon lost at the fair. His judgment was out there somewhere, he was sure, circling around like an angry crow, but he felt as free as the last man on Earth. He leered at the Hooter Girls with their copious bosoms and cantilevered asses, breasts pointed eagerly outward like the outstretched arms of a revival preacher, welcoming, warming. They wanted him to think they liked him, and by God they were succeeding.

Rolling toward home on the Interstate, Tubby dialed his ex-wife on the car phone.

"Is that you, Tubby?"

"Yeah, can't you hear me?"

"There's a little static. Are you calling me from your damn car phone?"

"Yeah. You called me?"

"We need to talk, and not on the phone. Has Christine spoken to you about her trip to Europe?"

"First I heard of it."

"What did you say? You're breaking up."

"I just went under a bridge. I said, first I heard of it."

"It's going to cost four thousand dollars, Tubby."

"I don't think that's going to be a problem."

"What, Tubby? Are you doing something to that phone deliberately?"

Tubby was holding it out the window. He pulled his arm back in. "Mattie, I'll drop by."

"Did you say you're coming over?"

"Yes."

"When?"

"Right now."

"That's a surprise."

He hung up. One of life's unpleasantnesses was about to go away. Tubby hummed to the rock'n' roll oldies on the radio. As he exited on Carrollton he was singing and thumping the steering wheel in time to the music.

He rang the doorbell of the house on State Street, the house he and Mattie had shared for seventeen years and in which he had not lived for four years. She kept it up nice, he thought, but it could use a coat of paint soon. There were rust spots on the gutters in front with delicate ferns peeking through them. They had not been there when he left, he was damn sure of that.

She came to the door wearing baggy white shorts and a madras blouse, earrings, and a matching tennis ankle bracelet, so he knew she had dressed up a little for the occasion. Nothing surprising there. She would want him to know how well she was doing, physically and emotionally, to go along with how poorly she was doing financially.

Mattie was a head shorter than he was and had red hair and a tiny colony of freckles under each of her blue eyes. She had a big mouth, both figuratively and literally, which could break into the kind of smile that would make a state trooper tear up a ticket. The smile was the thing that had drawn him in years ago. That and her gorgeous tits, to be honest about it. But it was her way of always staying a step ahead of him in a conversation that kept him around. She was getting a little plump, but all in all, with three kids, she was looking pretty good.

The first thing that hit him whenever he saw her was how long they had been happily, he thought, married, and how short had been the period of dissatisfaction before the divorce. Yet the years of their marriage, and the birthing and raising of children, were such a blur in his memory, and it seemed there were only a few fragments he could bring back clearly. But the painful days blasted back into his consciousness whenever they felt like it, and there was no on-off switch for them. After Tubby moved out, Mattie had taken her trips and had her affair, at least one that Tubby knew about, under circumstances he had found embarrassing and hard to forgive. When it was clear that their temporary separation would be permanent, when they both settled into their new and private lifestyles, the trauma finally passed. Now they had healed their own wounds as best they could, but Tubby knew that his were still close to the surface, waiting around.

"Hi, Mattie." He pecked her on the cheek as she tilted toward him.

"Come on back." She led the way to the kitchen. It was

done in white and black tiles, which he had paid for, and a tiled bar where they used to eat their family meals together.

"Would you like a drink?" she asked.

"Are you having one?"

"Just a little glass of wine."

"If you've got some bourbon, I'll have some with soda."

"You never were a soda drinker."

"Hey, I'm getting sophisticated." Actually he was getting drunk.

"Where are the girls?" he asked.

"Christine is in Florida. Collette is going to a party and may sleep over at her friend's tonight. Debbie is probably at her apartment, but she may drop in later."

She organized the drinks efficiently, placed his on the counter, and moved around to the other side to perch on a stool.

"What's this about Europe?" he asked.

"Christine has a chance to go with her Newman class for a month to Paris, and then to Italy. Everybody attends language classes, and they take bicycle trips and, you know, travel around. It's going to cost about four thousand dollars for her tickets and tuition and some spending money. They'll be staying in youth hostels, but even so . . ."

"Four grand," he said as he sipped.

"I spoke to Vinny about it, and he thinks it's covered in the decree." Vinny was her lawyer, and here was where Tubby was supposed to get nervous and angry. He was sure Vinny had told her no such thing, but this was the tip-off that the tough negotiating was about to begin.

"I don't think four thousand will be a problem, Mattie.

Let's take care of it now." He pulled a long envelope out of the breast pocket of his jacket and counted out $4,000 in $100s onto the bar. He pushed it over to her. "I want her to have a good time."

Mattie did not speak right away, which gratified Tubby a lot. Plus, from her little half smile he could see she was really pleased. She liked to argue, especially about money, but she liked money more.

"Why, Tubby, that's so sweet. Where did it all come from?"

"Lucky day at the track."

"I'm so surprised. I thought this was going to be one of those long-drawn-out fights." She came around the bar and kissed him on the forehead. Tubby inhaled the familiar perfume she wore on her neck and shoulders, and couldn't keep from beaming.

"I also brought you a little extra," he said. "I know I've been slow a couple of months." He pinched a half inch of bills from the envelope and pressed them into her hand. Such joy from soft, green rag paper, smelling of fingers and printer's ink and leather wallets, a richness like fresh turned soil. Mattie's mouth formed a perfect O as she stared at the warm pile in her hand. She was moved, deeply.

"Oh, Tubby, this is not necessary," like he had given her a present on their first date.

He gave her the old smile and wink.

She bent over, and this time the kiss was on the lips. Tubby himself continued to float somewhere overhead, watching it all happen, from his golden balloon.

"Here's a little tip." Gently he slipped a few bills past the open neck of her blouse and tucked them into her bra.

Her face lit up, on fire. It was happy. She held his hand to her breast, then brought it inside, guiding his fingers to pull aside her blouse and pull down the bra covering her right breast till, pushed skyward by elastic, it pointed at his face.

"Why don't you kiss it, sweet little baby," she said. She pressed herself into his mouth, and he obliged, tasting old flavors. Slowly, with his free hand, he folded another bill and slid it into the band of her shorts.

The electricity was running full current. With her free hand she undid her eelskin belt and pulled down the zipper. He tucked more $100s into her sheer panties. She yanked his belt buckle loose, pulled her breast from his face, kissed him hard, then knelt on the tile floor. She unzipped his pants and worked him free. While she caressed him moistly, Tubby selected bills, one at a time, touched her delicately about the cheeks and neck with them and let them fall. They formed a ragged green carpet around his horny one-time wife. It really took so little to make everything good, really good.

THIRTEEN

TUBBY LEFT IN THE MORNING before she woke up. It was raining lightly outside, and the air was sweet. He expected Mattie would be embarrassed about what they had done. To a certain extent, he was, too. When it's over, it's supposed to be over. By pure luck, none of the girls had come home. The last thing they needed was some false hope that their parents were reconciling. It had taken them long enough to adapt to the breakup. He looked forward to taking a shower at his house and then going to work to find out what he had missed during his shopping spree yesterday. There were still living clients to care about, and Tubby's guiding principle was never screw a client.

He left the money in the trunk of his car, not being able to think of a better place for it. After packing the smaller presents he had bought into a sock drawer, he showered, then fixed himself a cup of coffee, sliced up two satsumas, and ate the fruit. He locked up and drove downtown. He was in traffic on Claiborne Avenue when his car phone beeped.

"Mr. Dubonnet, this is Cherrylynn." Her voice was almost hysterical. "Someone broke into the office last night."

"How do you know?"

"It's a mess. The files are everywhere. Your desk drawer was broken open. The safe is open. They went through my desk. And Mr. Turntide's office is torn up, too."

"Are the police there?"

"Not yet. But I called them. Mr. Turntide told me to. They should be here soon."

"Right. Some ace detectives, I'll bet."

"Only in the movies. But really, Mr. Dubonnet, you had better come down here. It really is a wreck."

"I'm already headed that way."

The police had arrived when he got to the office. Or rather, a lone officer in uniform was shaking his head over the carnage. The place was pretty much as Cherrylynn had described it. Files were dumped everywhere—on the floor, on the desks, in the hall. Books had been pulled off their shelves. His globe had been overturned. He was sad to see that his leather chair had been ripped open and the stuffing was pulled out. Mattie had given him the chair for Christmas when he first started practicing law. It was accustomed to his backside now and fit him just right. Worst of all, one of the oil paintings on the wall, an abstract by the local artist Still, had been slashed. The artist was also his client, but Tubby had actually paid money for the painting because he admired it so much. He liked it when people studied it and was proud to say that he knew the painter. It was going to be expensive as hell to fix.

Reggie and Cherrylynn went with the policeman into the relative normalcy of the kitchen to talk. Tubby followed after them.

"I can't believe what they did to your office, Tubby," Reggie said. "What could they have been after?"

Tubby shook his head.

"They sure got your office a lot worse than mine."

"It's just devastating," moaned Cherrylynn.

"Come look at mine," Reggie said. They walked down the hall through the litter. The wreckage here was on a smaller scale.

Reggie lowered his voice. "This is pretty intense, Tubby. What's going on?"

"I don't know."

"Are you working on anything that could, you know, lead to this?"

"Not that I know of."

"You think it could be connected with Darryl Alvarez?"

"How do you mean?"

"I don't know. You tell me. Drugs? Money? Did he leave anything with you?" Reggie's eyebrows twitched.

"No." Being partners didn't mean you had to tell each other everything.

"All of my clients are regular businessmen, Tubby."

Sure, thought Tubby. "Does that make them sweethearts?" he asked.

Reggie blinked rapidly, maybe thinking. "It's not really their style," he said. "Plus, whoever heard of busting up a lawyer's office just because you're mad at him? This doesn't look like vandalism to me. You better go over your client list, Tubby."

"You can bet I'll give it some thought." Tubby meant that. "Guess we better call the insurance company."

Cherrylynn came and got them. The policeman wanted an inventory. She also told Tubby that Clifford Banks was on the phone. Banks was the chairman of the Louisiana Bond Counsel Association. He represented municipalities and parish governments wishing to sell tax-free securities. He was known throughout the state. He never called Tubby Dubonnet, and Tubby tried to steer clear of guys like Clifford Banks.

"I'll tell him you'll call him later."

"Right. No. I'll take it at my desk."

He had to look for the phone. It was on the floor, underneath a pile of paper, but it was still plugged in. Cherrylynn had been picking up and reshelving books, but she stepped outside to give him some privacy.

"Hello, Mr. Dubonnet?" It was a quiet, assured voice. A flat, slightly nasal accent. A Republican Garden District voice.

"Yes."

"I'm sorry to call you out of the blue like this. It's been quite some time since we were introduced at the Federal Bar Association dinner." Tubby had only the faintest recollection of attending any such dinner. He thought it might have been two or three years ago. He did not recall that Clifford Banks had been in attendance, though you shook so many hands at those affairs that anything was possible.

"I didn't think you'd remember that," Tubby said lamely.

"Of course I do. Listen, I'll tell you why I called. I have a client who is interested in the death of Darryl Alvarez."

"Uh-huh."

"He is a potential heir to Mr. Alvarez's estate, and he is trying to learn more about the circumstances of his death, and what the assets of the estate are, things of that nature."

"I wouldn't know about either, Clifford," Tubby said, but he was thinking that the other shoe was finally beginning to drop. "I was just representing him on a criminal matter. I don't even know if he left a will. Who is your client?"

"I'm afraid I'm not at liberty to say. I know a statement like that always raises more questions than anything else, and I assure you there is nothing to hide here, but I have to respect my client's wishes."

"I don't see how I can help you."

"You may be able to help me more than you think. I wonder if I might meet with you, this afternoon if possible, and perhaps I can explain a little more fully what I'm trying to find out. Could I drop by your office?"

"No, I'm sorry, but my office is being remodeled right now." Tubby righted a trashcan with his foot and tried to collect the wadded-up things that had spilled from it.

"Then perhaps you could drop by mine," Banks said. "Or, better still, why not let me buy you a drink after work. We could meet in the bar at the Fairmont."

Tubby had no desire to meet with him anytime, but he said, "Okay, what time?"

"Whatever suits you. How about six o'clock?"

"All right, I'll see you there."

Tubby hung up and looked around his office. The cabinet safe wasn't bank-vault quality, but someone had to know what they were doing to get it open. He had no doubt that the safe was the target. The burglar or burglars had probably cut up the oil painting and his chair just out of meanness. He walked outside and found the policeman sitting at Cherrylynn's reception desk, writing up his report. He was tall and good-looking and very young. Cherrylynn was fawning over him. Tubby saw that the policeman had a cup of coffee, which his secretary must have fixed. The cop's radio was on, bleating announcements of car accidents interspersed with static.

"Do you know what you are missing, Mr. Dubonnet?"

"Not yet." Tubby gestured at the wreckage.

"Do you have any idea who might have done this?"

"Not a clue. Probably some doper."

"They would have taken your typewriters, and your curtains and your paper clips. Angry client?"

"I don't think I've made any that angry. Why don't you take some fingerprints or something?"

"I don't know what we'd print. A lot of people probably come in here. To be honest, we can't get the fingerprint teams out on anything but homicides or rapes. It's a question of resources."

"How do you ever catch anybody?"

"Well, you know, somebody turns them in, or, if something was stolen, it usually turns up. Also people confess. You're not sure that anything was stolen?"

"I'll know better when I clean up the mess. But really there's not much here to steal except the copier and the word processor, and they're still here."

The cop looked around as if to confirm that, nodded his head, and went back to writing.

"You find something gone, you call me," he said. "And if you need a report for your insurance company, here's the incident number." He tore off a slip of paper from his notebook and gave it to Tubby.

"And you call me if you learn anything or get a line on who might have done this."

Wasn't that supposed to be the other way around? Tubby asked himself.

"I will, Officer." He bent over to read the man's badge. Tucker. "I hear anything I'll call you."

"Okay, and thanks. See you later, ma'am," he said to Cherrylynn.

"Such a nice fellow," she said when he was out the door.

"Very easygoing," said Tubby. "Look, can you clean up this mess? I mean put the files in order. Call Maintenance and they can haul out the trash. I've got to get to court." He couldn't stand being there any longer, for some reason, and he needed to see Judge Hughes.

FOURTEEN

Monique WENT INTO mourning after Darryl got killed, but she managed to get the saloon back in operation. There was nothing official about it, but she had the keys and knew the combination to the safe, which nobody else did, so they all deferred to her. One night her apartment was ransacked while she was working, but she didn't report it. She just cleaned up the mess and went on. At least they didn't steal her bike. A man called her on the phone right after the shooting. She thought she recognized the voice as the guy on the balcony, the one with Casey who ordered a Wild Turkey.

"Where's the goddamn money?" was all he wanted to know.

She screamed incoherently into the phone long after he hung up. She did not have the fucking money, and did not know what Darryl had done with the fucking money, and did not care about the fucking money.

She began spending most of her time at the club. Except

for Ali, the bouncer where she used to work in the French Quarter, she really didn't have any other friends or much else to do. Even during her off hours she was usually upstairs in the office, exploring Darryl's life. She studied the ledgers and some spiral notebooks she discovered in the safe, and got a pretty good idea about the nuts and bolts of the operation—what went into the bank and what went into the cash box. She left the bag of pot and the ornate silver cocaine server where she found them in Darryl's desk. For some reason she wasn't much interested in dope anymore, but she still would take a drink. The employees got paid, so they were no problem. Her first challenge came from the whiskey wholesaler who showed up with his truck on Thursday morning, his usual time, and who said he wanted to deal "with the boss, now that Mr. Alvarez ain't here no more."

"I guess that's me," Monique told him.

"Who's going to be taking care of my bills?" he asked.

"I will. You'll get paid just like always. Just send me the invoice."

"Invoice, shit. Who's in charge here?" he demanded. "Where's the man?"

That made her mad. "I'm the one in charge," she said. "Now let's get those bottles unloaded."

The man got back in his truck and slammed the door. He started the motor. Then he rolled down the window and said, grinding his gears, "If you're in charge, you've got a lot to learn."

"Wait," Monique cried. She hopped up on the running board and got her face up to a level with his. It wasn't a pretty sight. She gripped the window frame with both hands, not planning to let him get away without her. "We need that stock. You can't just drive away."

"Like hell I can't," he said. "Let go of my truck."

"Tell me what the problem is. I don't understand."

He stared at her. "You got to know the deal. You can't run no bar if you don't know the deal."

"Okay, so explain it to me. What's the deal?"

The deal turned out to be very elaborate. Darryl paid the full inflated amount of each invoice by check. The liquor company paid a salary to Jimmy, the Champs bartender. Jimmy kicked back the money to Darryl, in cash. Darryl turned over part of the cash to the boss of the liquor company and kept part for himself. The way it worked out, the wholesaler's costs were covered, the bar got liquor, everybody's books balanced, and both bosses pocketed a little cash. And the driver usually delivered an extra case not shown on the invoice. And he deducted two bottles for his trouble.

"And you give me a gift certificate for a fifty-dollar dinner for my mom and papa's anniversary every year," he told her.

Maybe he made that last one up. Monique would never know.

"Sounds fine to me," she said and stuck out her hand. The driver smiled and took it. "How about unloading my whiskey?" she asked.

"Yes, ma'am. What you need extra today? I got Puerto Rican rum or Taaka vodka."

She asked Jimmy about the setup later. "Sure, that's the way it works," he said. "I thought you knew about it."

"I didn't know all the details," she told him.

"And when I cash the check, I take twenty dollars out as a tip." His expression radiated sincerity.

"I may let you up it to forty dollars," she said. "Are there any other deals you want to fill me in on?"

And so it went with the purveyors of food, napkins, toilet paper, toothpicks, and peppermints. Monique started to master the finer parts of running a business for the enjoyment of the public.

She took to sleeping in the office, or on the couch in the lounge. Sometimes Jimmy would lock up while she slept, and she would come awake before dawn, the club strangely empty and silent, wondering where she was. Then she would hear the lake sounds normally muffled by the noises of the crowd—the waves lapping at the rocks, the cool wind from the north, the chimes of rigging ringing against the aluminum masts of the sailboats—and she would remember.

Then she would go downstairs and walk around in the dark and stand on the spot on the floor where Darryl had bled to death. And she would take a tall glass from the wooden rack inside the bar and fill it half full of vodka and the rest of the way full with cranberry and orange juice mixed, and she would sit on one of the stools and smoke cigarettes by herself, waiting for the sun to come up so that she could know where the water ended and the land began.

She was waiting like that, sitting behind the bar in the dark and staring over the stacked chairs at a blank picture window just starting to shift from ebony to charcoal gray, when she heard a scratching noise from the direction of the front door. At first she thought it might be a rat. There were a few about, a fact she had learned since she had started sleeping over. She had made the help set out extra traps. But it wasn't a rat, she realized, when she heard the front door swing open with a creak and felt a little gust of fresh air pass around the bar. A napkin in the clear plastic box beside her blew onto the floor.

She concentrated on the space where the front hallway met the barroom. Her eyes were used to the night, and she watched alertly for movement and shadows. In a few seconds she saw the figure of a man framed by the entranceway. He moved silently in her direction, pausing with each step to listen. Monique reached for the gun under the register. She got it in her left hand and transferred it to her right without leaving the stool. The man must have sensed the movement because he crouched.

"Who's there?" he said in a low voice, like he wasn't totally sure that anyone was there. She recognized the voice as Casey's.

"Me," she said, and with both hands folded around the pearly grips, she focused what she had at his shadow and started shooting.

"Shit!" Casey yelled and tumbled onto the floor. A table loaded with chairs turned over with a crash. Casey fired a weapon—she saw the flash but had no thought about where the bullet went—then, with a leap, he smashed through the window she had been looking through and rolled outside. She heard his footsteps running away on the dock.

Monique stood frozen, both arms extended, pointing her pistol at the broken window, for a minute or more, and then she sat down on the floor.

"Where's the damn police?" she sobbed. Not even a dog barked. None lived by the lake. Just the rigging banging on the masts.

"Where are the sirens?" she cried.

She got up and walked around the room, stepping around tables and looking into corners. She stuck her head through the jagged hole in the window and looked at the trees blowing outside. A breeze picked up a Popeye's bag and blew it down the street. She rubbed her hands over the pistol. She smelled its barrel. Somewhere there was a rat in here. At least she could blow that away. An orange streak split the sky.

The sun came up. Monique sat outside on the dock, watching seagulls dive for their breakfast of minnows at the mouth of the harbor. She was in the company of a bottle of vodka and a row of orange juice cans. The Baretta 9 was on the plank beside her, glistening with dew. She hadn't thought about it for a while, and didn't know if it still held any bullets. Some early morning fishermen set up their gear on the rocks across the channel. One waved at her, and in a minute she waved back.

She got on her feet, not smoothly, stretched, and went back inside to use the phone. It rang a long time before she heard her mama say hello.

"Hello, Mama."

"Who is this? Monique?"

"Yes, Mama."

"What are you calling so early for?"

"I just got up early this morning. I thought you'd be awake by now. Is Lisa all right?"

"Of course she's all right. What makes you think she wouldn't be all right? Where are you?"

"I'm in New Orleans, Mama. I just wanted to hear your voice and talk to Lisa."

"You sound real funny, Monique, like you're in a dream. Have you been drinking?"

"No, Mama. I just had a real bad night. Is Lisa there?"

"She's here and in bed and that's where I'm going to leave her. It's too early in the morning to be making a phone call and waking people up."

"I know she'd like to talk to me."

"No, she wouldn't. It would just trouble her right now. And you've been enough trouble to her already. I'm going to leave her asleep."

"Please, Mama."

"Monique, quit saying please this and please that. You get yourself back together first, and then we'll talk about it."

Monique couldn't think of anything else to say.

"Okay, Mama. Well, then I guess I'll let you go. You'll tell her I called, won't you?"

"Yes, but I won't tell her how you sounded."

"Goodbye, Mama."

"Goodbye."

FIFTEEN

"TUBBY, WHATSA BIG DEAL, huh? You just droppin' in or what?" Judge Hughes gave Tubby's hand a mighty shake.

"I was just in the neighborhood, Al, and I thought I'd see if you were real busy."

"Gawd, yes. It's always real busy. You see all those guys out there? That's two pretrials and a temporary restraining order. Then I got a trial resuming at two o'clock."

Judge Hughes always smiled when he talked, so he looked kind of like a brown cherub because he was bald and had a round, plump face, big inquisitive eyes, and curly ears. Being a judge, you would think he had heard everything, but he always looked like he was curious about what you were going to say. He was invariably friendly and courteous to lawyers, though slow as molasses to render a judgment and sometimes hard to get on the bench. He much preferred meeting in chambers with just the lawyers around, to get it all arranged peacefully. He was probably Tubby's oldest friend in the city.

They had studied together in law school. The bond was firmed up when they had both clerked at the district attorney's office and realized that they both regarded their boss, a flamboyant DA who always found fiction more persuasive than fact, ridiculous, not to say dangerous. Hughes was one of the first blacks to make a serious run for Civil District Court, and Tubby had walked him around to meet a lot of the white lawyers in town.

"I can get out of your hair," Tubby said.

"No, let them suffer. I need a breather. That's why I told Mrs. Carlozzi to bring you on in. So what's new?"

"I got a little problem."

"What kind of problem? How can I help you?"

"It's an ethical problem. It seems I've got something I don't own, and I'm not sure who it belongs to."

The judge leaned back in his chair. "So what is it?" he asked.

"You don't want to know. Well, maybe later, but not now."

"So you keep it, what's the problem? After a while it's yours by acquisitive prescription."

"There may not be a problem. I don't think anybody has a legitimate claim to it, at least not better than my claim. The police might like to know about it. I don't know for sure."

"You mean it's involved in a crime?"

"I wouldn't be surprised, but I don't know that."

"Are the police looking for it?"

"Not so far as I know, and I doubt it."

"They haven't asked you for it."

"Certainly not."

"So what's the big deal? If the police want something, they're not shy, they'll ask for it. If they don't ask, fuck them."

"That's about where I'm coming out."

"If nobody's asking for it, and you don't know who it belongs to, keep it."

"Okay."

"Hypothetically speaking, of course." The judge grinned.

"Right. I realize you don't have all the facts."

"Just declare it on your income tax so you don't get Uncle on your tail."

"Hmmm."

"So what else you got?"

"I got this urge to proposition my daughter's sixteen-year-old girlfriend. Is that all right? No, just kidding. I think that's about it. I'll be going."

"I saw Mattie at the Gibsons' party," the judge said. "She looked good. Divorcing you seems to have agreed with her."

"Yeah. I saw her this week. She is looking good."

"Let's have lunch one day."

"Okay, Al, maybe Friday. I'll be kind of busy until then."

"Call me Friday morning."

"You got it."

Tubby rose from his chair and started out, but Judge Hughes held up a hand to stop him.

"Do you know what I tell judges from all over the country when I go to the Bar Association meetings and all those judicial conferences?"

"No, what?" Tubby asked.

"I tell them to come to New Orleans to see the prettiest girls in the world, do you agree?"

"Sure," Tubby said.

"Well," said the judge, getting up and stretching. He came around his desk to face Tubby. "You may or may not actually agree, but if you count the Vietnamese girls and the brown girls and the white girls and the black girls, you know I'm right. Just look around you. And what makes them so pretty is that they smile. I don't know if it's what we put in the water or what. In New Orleans, the girls smile. That's why they're so beautiful." He squeezed Tubby's arm. "You've got to keep smiling, Tubby. That's my moral. And on your way out would you ask Mrs. Carlozzi to send in the TRO."

"Sure, see you Al."

Tubby made it to the Central Grocery before it closed, double-parked, and picked up a can of olive oil and a large sack of pistachios. The olive oil was for cooking and the pistachio nuts were for writing briefs. Since he'd started doing all of his own shopping and cooking, he ate much better things.

After he got his groceries, he drove around the French Quarter to the old D. H. Holmes department store parking garage on Iberville Street. You parked your own car and took the keys with you. With almost a million dollars in the trunk, he was not about to turn the wheel over to some kid. Also it was rush hour, and he didn't want to get tied up in business-district traffic driving across Canal to the Fairmont parking lot. It was just a short walk to the hotel.

The Fairmont's narrow lobby ran the length of the block.

Since they tore down the St. Charles, this was really the only one of the grand hotels left. Carnival's first royalty held court here, though they called it the Grunewald then, and Huey Long plotted upstairs to beat the New Orleans machine. The scheme for his famous "Round Robin," which scuttled his impeachment, was hatched upstairs, so they said, and in a nearby room his assassins may have met secretly to plan his death.

It was orderly and sedate, a nice contrast to his office, which he had spent the afternoon helping to reorganize. Nothing had turned up missing. That was probably because what the burglars were looking for was in the trunk of his car.

Sazerac's was the bar off the lobby. Tubby usually avoided it because it was likely to be full of conventioneers, but tonight, except for a couple of cigar chompers and the bartender, the place was dead.

He recognized Clifford Banks sitting at a round table in a dim corner beneath an orange mural, painted by a WPA artist, of vegetable and fruit vendors in the French Market. Banks was smoking a cigarette, but he stubbed it out as soon as Tubby entered the room. He placed the ashtray surreptitiously on the adjoining table like he was ashamed of it. When he stood up to shake hands, Tubby had to acknowledge that he had a commanding presence. With streaks of silver at his temples, and his wide, clear blue eyes, he was a distinguished figure.

"Hello, Tubby," he said. His voice was generous and friendly. "Thank you for joining me."

"My pleasure, Clifford." Tubby fitted himself into one of the soft black leather chairs. They contrasted with the rug, the curtains, and the base of the bar, which were red, like dark blood. A waiter appeared. Banks ordered a martini, straight up, please, dry with an olive. Tubby said he would have the same. A speaker hidden somewhere emitted Stravinsky. Or maybe it was drifting in from the symphony playing at the Orpheum across the street.

"I don't think I've seen you since the Bar dinner a year or so ago," Banks said. "But I've heard you have been doing very well."

"I've been staying busy." The waiter brought mixed nuts.

"That's certainly better than the alternative." Banks chuckled. Tubby smiled. They smiled at each other.

The drinks came. Banks fiddled with his red plastic swizzle stick. It was imprinted with the Fairmont Hotel crest and would have been something to grab for if it was tossed from a float at Mardi Gras.

"Tubby, you may be able to help me," he began. Tubby didn't say anything but raised his eyebrows and tried to look cooperative. It was an effort to avoid staring at Clifford's tie, a collage of purple plums on a cloudy pink sky.

"I've got a client who is interested in certain assets of Darryl Alvarez. Would you have any idea what I'm talking about?"

"Why don't you tell me," he said.

Banks seemed to ponder this and took a moment to respond. He tried again.

"I believe it's cash, Tubby, a sizeable amount of cash."

"Where did you get the idea that Alvarez had a sizeable amount of cash?" Tubby asked.

Banks nodded. "It could have been in a blue gym bag, Tubby. Alvarez didn't give you anything like that, did he?"

"Whose money was it?"

"My client's. And he is very anxious to have it back."

"Why doesn't he go to the police?"

"He would prefer to leave it a private matter."

"What does that have to do with me?"

"I hoped, Tubby, that you would help us find it, and give it back."

"Why in hell should I do that?"

"Because in fairness, and as compensation for your efforts, you would be entitled to be rewarded for your time, and because you could help us to avoid an unpleasant situation."

"What does that mean?"

"I suppose I mean the unpleasantness of my client not getting his money."

"I don't see how I can help you unless you tell me whom you represent or who claims the cash."

Banks again paused before he spoke. He consulted his cocktail napkin and mopped up a ring on the table. "Tubby, give it back," he whispered. His eyes came up and latched on to Tubby's.

"I don't think I want to continue this conversation. I'll be leaving now." Tubby got up, nodded to Banks, and walked out.

"Sorry we couldn't do business," Banks said to his back.

Tubby did not see it, but Banks lit another cigarette as soon as Tubby was gone. He asked the bartender for a telephone.

Tubby walked back across Canal Street to the garage, glad to be outside. Iberville was not a busy street at night. In fact, it was downright deserted. He had to take a tiny elevator to "green," where his car was parked. As he got on, a tall guy in a T-shirt, shorts, and running shoes glided in with him. Tubby pressed the number of his floor and glanced at his fellow passenger. The man gave him a distant smile. He had a long scar on his cheek, which he probably thought was sexy, and a lot of muscles.

The elevator stopped on the third floor, and when Tubby stepped out the man came with him. Tubby did not like that, so he stopped to fish around in his pocket for his parking ticket. The man also stopped and looked at Tubby serenely.

"What do you want?" Tubby asked, having a hard time controlling his breathing.

"Let's get in your car, Mr. Dubonnet. Then you do what I say." The guy's voice was not unfriendly. He was at least a head taller than Tubby was.

"I don't think so," Tubby said, not very loudly.

The man with the scar reached behind him and pulled out a small handgun that must have been holstered somewhere in the band of his running shorts, and he held it out for Tubby to see. Tubby was reminded of a policeman showing a badge. The man was simply providing the explanation for why Tubby should do what he was told. The gun was very small, but Tubby knew it could cause pain. He was no longer into guns. He had seen a lot of their victims. Before he could react, the man with the scar suddenly grabbed Tubby's left ear and twisted it violently, bringing him to his knees.

"Let's go, little man," he hissed, and started pulling Tubby with him.

Just then the elevator door behind them whooshed open,

and a Hispanic couple stepped off. Tubby's ear was released in an instant, and the man palmed the gun.

"Excuse us," said the woman, a short, dark-haired figure with deep-set eyes. She was plainly irritated that her way was blocked by two men possibly fornicating.

Tubby started running. Faded arrows painted on the concrete showed the ramp down, and down he went. He looked over his shoulder to see three surprised faces, then saw the guy with the gun start running after him. Tubby was pumping hard, trying to keep his footing on the greasy driveway, coated with years of car exhaust and oil pan drippings. His hard-soled shoes kept sliding, and he had to push off the wall to avoid sprawling headfirst onto the cement. He heard sneakers behind him when he ran past the ticket booth and hit the street. He cut left, toward Bourbon, where there were tourists and lights. Behind him he heard a commotion when the man following him got tangled up with an old derelict who was weaving down the block. Then the sneakers pounded after him again.

On Bourbon Street the revelry was in high gear, and he ran straight into the crush. It carried him along toward the music. He was in a current of tourists and partygoers waving cups of beer and Hurricanes, small-towners pointing out freaks and laughing.

Tubby went with the flow, but tried to go a little faster than the rest of the crowd. He needed to catch his breath, and he was trying to find a cop. Once he looked back and he saw the face of the muscle man. It was no more than twenty-five feet away, grimly keeping pace.

The middle of the street was blocked by a ring of partyers

watching some black kids tap-dance with bottle caps nailed to their shoes, the sights of a primitive city. They kept time to the Dukes of Dixieland blasting away inside. Tubby pushed around them, feeling rather than seeing his pursuer. And then he picked out a policeman, a cop on a horse outside of a loud rock'n' roll club, talking to a few out-of-towners and posing for photographs. Tubby rushed up and patted the policeman's patent-leather riding boots, trying to get the cop's attention.

"Officer." He really had to squeeze the boot to get the man to look down. He gave Tubby an angry glare.

"Officer, there's a man following me. He's got a gun."

The cop leaned over to get a better look at Tubby. "Where is he?" he asked.

Tubby pointed back in the direction he had come, but the guy had faded away.

"He was right there."

"Do you know who it was?"

"No."

"What did he look like?"

"White male, real tall, over six feet, wearing jogging shorts and a T-shirt." Tubby and the policeman scanned the crowd. A lot of the people on the street looked sort of like that.

The policeman pulled his walkie-talkie off his belt and relayed the information to someone unseen.

"We'll look for him," he said to Tubby.

"Thank you, Officer," Tubby said. Then he hung around, not sure what he was supposed to do next. The policeman stood up in his stirrups and looked around a little bit more. Then a pretty girl asked him where Pat O'Brien's was, and then begged him to let her take his picture with her girl-friend holding the bridle. Tubby began feeling a little dumb just being there. People kept bumping into him. There wasn't anyplace to sit.

Maybe he could find a cab across the street from Antoine's, he thought. Carefully looking around, he stepped back into the tourist flow. There was a row of cabs on St. Louis, down the block from the famous restaurant. Their drivers were sitting under a tall magnolia, drinking from plastic cups and playing dominoes. Tubby moved into the light with them, under a street lamp swarming with moths and lovebugs.

"Uptown?" he asked, addressing the lounging drivers in general.

"Taxi, here, sir." A big fellow slid off the wall. "Finish for me, Ice Man," he said to a skinny guy seated cross-legged on the grass, who took his place at the game. The driver opened the door of an old Cadillac painted white. Tubby got into the backseat quickly.

"I'm going, too." The man with the scar pushed in behind Tubby. Tubby kept on going, pulling the far door latch and popping out the other side of the cab.

"Shit. Hey, what?" the cabdriver cried.

Tubby was running again, but on dark streets now, near-ing Jackson Square. He rounded a corner into an alleyway beside the dark cathedral, looking wildly for a weapon or someplace to hide. Some loose old bricks were piled against the granite wall of the church, which a wino had probably used for a seat. Tubby picked one up and pressed himself against the wall. When the scarred man ran around the corner, Tubby hit him with it full in the face. He felt something squash, and blood sprayed out like beer foam.

The man went down on his back, and Tubby kicked him in the groin. The man tried to curl up, but he was passing out. Tubby kicked him again, then stomped again and again on his head. Finally he got control of himself. The man's face looked like a spit-out wad of chewing tobacco. He no longer had a scar, and he wasn't moving. A hundred feet away, at the far end of the dark alleyway, silhouetted against the lights of Jackson Square, a well-dressed couple were frozen in place, trying to understand what they were looking at. The pigeons in the church eaves above fluttered and cooed. Tubby began to run again, away from the Square. "Get off the street, get where it's air-conditioned, get a drink." In that order, Tubby commanded himself.

He stumbled into the back entrance of the Royal Orleans and leaned against the mirrored wall to catch his breath. Nobody was around. He studied his own face and tried to compose it into something he recognized. Thanking God for his Visa Gold Card, he limped upstairs to the front desk.

He was shown to a room near the top. Room service brought him a pitcher of martinis. From his window he had a sweeping view of the lights of the Quarter and the black void that was Lake Pontchartrain beyond that. He left the curtain wide open because he needed the feel of space. He was not afraid so high up. After a while the alcohol began to take effect. Such an experience makes drinking respectable, he was sure. This was a lot deeper than he had planned to go. Life was a very nice thing to have, and money could not replace it. He had bought his little trinkets and taken care of a few pressing domestic details. Time to get off this train. Tubby fell asleep in his chair, his feet on the bed. He jerked and his glass fell to the rug, ice and whiskey melting into the carpet. An olive rolled under the window curtain, where it waited to surprise the next guest.

He dreamed that his friends were with him. Jason Boaz, the inventor, was there. So was E. J. Chaisson. So was Reggie Turntide. They were playing soldier in the rice fields around Bunkie, but it wasn't a game after all because the guns were real. They were on their stomachs, taking cover behind a low dirt levee pushed up by a grader to hold water in the fields. The water was rising, and already it was covering the green shoots of the young plants and soaking into their boots. His partner, Reggie, was crawling through the mud, his arms wrapped around the gym bag. They were receiving mortar fire but could not tell where it came from. Enemies were crawling through the rice like alligators. The ground was exploding and dirt was showering down, covering them. Jason rigged up an irrigation pump to a fat fire hose. E.J. opened a bottle of wine and poured it, red and thick, into a cracked glass. He handed it around like a communion cup.

"Here's to filthy lucre," he said, and they drank.

It was good to be among friends. Jason rose up, exposing himself to fire, and sprayed the enemy with clouds of flame erupting from his hose. But the wind blew it back on them. Everything, the rice fields, all his friends, were burning up. He had to get them out of there alive, or else he'd be all alone.

SIXTEEN

TUBBY WOKE UP ALONE, uncomfortable and chilly in an armchair in a strange room. He checked out, a wrinkled, unshaven version of the guest who had arrived, and got a sniff from the desk clerk. Tubby was feeling groggy and painfully stiff, and he paid no attention. He took a taxi back to the Holmes garage and asked the driver to take him all the way to his car. The man obliged and got a little something extra for his trouble. He watched until Tubby got his car started, then followed him out. Nothing bad happened.

Tubby waved the taxi away and drove home. Everything looked normal from the outside. The morning paper was on the steps. Tubby picked it up and went inside. Nothing seemed to be out of place. He showered and shaved, took some Tylenol, and wandered around the house with a towel wrapped around his waist. The housekeeper wasn't due until around eleven o'clock, and he would be dressed by then. He poured some tomato juice and swallowed his vitamins.

He thumbed through the white pages, then used the wall phone in the kitchen to place a call.

"Hello. This is Tubby Dubonnet. Is Clifford Banks in, please?"

The secretary doubted it, but she was wrong.

"Why, hello, Tubby. How are you?" He seemed genuinely concerned.

"I'll survive. I've located the asset you were looking for."

"That's wonderful. I was afraid I wouldn't hear from you."

"Yeah, and I'd like to turn it over to its rightful owner. Is that you?"

"Absolutely not. I just represent the owner."

"I'll bring it to you, then. I have to be in court for a couple of hours, then I'll come to your office."

"No, that's not a good idea. I think my client will have to handle that directly."

"Okay, where can I meet him?"

"Let me call you back on that, Tubby."

"Let's make it soon."

"Time is always of the essence, isn't it?"

Tubby hung up. He stared into his tomato juice for a moment, considered fortifying it with vodka, but he did not. He had to see a judge, and one of his little rules was always do that sober.

Eddie Rodrigue and George Guyoz were killing time in the narrow hallway leading to Judge Maselli's chambers. Between them and the door was the judge's secretary, an ancient gray-haired lady with the eye and carriage of a vulture, generally regarded by lawyers of all sexes as one of the biggest bitches in the courthouse. Behind her back you could refer to her as "The Bitch" and everybody knew who you were talking about, but to her face you called her Mrs. Maselli, since she was the judge's mother.

"Tubby, howya doin'?" asked Rodrigue in a syrupy sing-song that was his trademark. He was a soprano on the "Howya" and a baritone on the "doin.' " Eddie was a state representative from Westwego, and one of the friendliest men in New Orleans. He had a lot of silver hair, which he wore combed up bouffant-style like Liberace. His role in the Sandy Shandell lawsuit was zero. He represented Dr. Feingold's excess insurer, the insurance company that would have to pay off any claims over $10,000,000. There was no way that Sandy was ever going to win that much, but Tubby had sued all of Dr. Feingold's insurance companies on the theory that the more bags of money you got together, the more chances that one of them would spring a leak. It meant that Eddie was getting paid to come to court and shake hands, which suited him fine.

Guyoz, by contrast, represented Feingold's primary liability insurer, and his company would have to ante up whatever the jury awarded, minus the doctor's deductible, of course. Guyoz always looked like there was something sour in his mouth. He had a neat toothbrush mustache, and reminded Tubby of Adolf Hitler. He did not seem to have much sense of humor, and none at all about this lawsuit, which did have comic possibilities.

"All right, Eddie. How you been?"

"Very fine, Tubby. Everything is just fine. Business is good."

Tubby said hello to Guyoz, and got a nod and a throat-clearing in reply.

"Where's the judge?" he asked Eddie.

"He's on the bench, but he keeps slipping back to his office. There's some unfair trade practices trial going on, and Mrs. Maselli here," Eddie smiled at Mrs. Maselli, "just told me they are reading forty-seven depositions to the jury. Can you believe that? Forty-seven depositions."

"You're kidding me." Tubby cracked open the side door to the courtroom and, sure enough, a lawyer at a podium was slowly reading questions from a transcript to another lawyer playing the role of the witness, who tonelessly read the answers from the same script to twelve jurors in various stages of catatonia. The judge had his face covered by his hands like he was weeping at a funeral. Boredom had driven off any spectators, but there were at least ten attorneys at the counsel table, staring off into space. One was surreptitiously reading a magazine folded on his knees.

Tubby shut the door. "How long has this been going on?" he asked.

"Mrs. Maselli says for two days, and one more day to go."

"How do you suppose they stay awake?"

"They don't. Hey, did you ever hear this story? Did you ever know Vick Borzey? He was Judge Christmas's clerk for maybe twenty years. I think he's retired now. Anyway, the judge is on the bench, and Fred Boudreau, or one of the lawyers with him, is examining this witness. It's a maritime case. It's dragging on, and they've just had their lunch break. Everybody's sleepy, and Vick, you know, nods out. Boudreau asks the witness a question, and the other side's lawyer cries out 'Objection.' Vick, the clerk, jerks his head up and yells, 'Overruled.' Judge Christmas holds up his hand and gets everybody up to the bench. 'Victor,' he says, 'that ain't your job. I'm the one who gets to rule on the objections.' " Eddie let out a whinny.

"That's funny," Tubby said. "No, I never heard about that. Vick must have been dreaming he was the judge."

"Don't we all, Tubby?"

"Not me. I couldn't stand the tedium."

"Sugar!" The judge's voice boomed from his office. The Bitch jumped up—spry for a lady of advanced years—and pranced past the lawyers with her habitual triumphant sneer, like she had just beaten everybody in the room in some contest.

"Yes, Judge," she said when she disappeared inside. A moment later she stuck her head back out and asked whether everyone was present for the Sandy Shandell pretrial. Eddie said they were all here, and she told them to come on back into chambers.

Judge Maselli was no intellectual wiz, nor was he especially hardworking. His day began late and ended early. Real court was held at the restaurant at the Warwick Hotel down the street, where he ate breakfast and lunch and enjoyed the afternoon happy hour, often in the company of lawyers who had cases on his docket. He held conferences in his chambers as rarely as possible because his mother was there. He genuinely appreciated her ability to manage that aspect of his life, but preferred to be elsewhere while she did it. Still, local rules of court adopted by his fellow judges required assembling lawyers shortly before trial to hash out details and arguments and, most importantly, to try to compel a settlement that would avoid trial. Already it took three or more years to get a jury trial. Without settlements it would take twenty.

Maselli was scowling at the pretrial memoranda he was reading when the lawyers filed in and said, "Good morning, Your Honor." They took seats in front of his massive desk like pupils at the feet of some great sage. The judge was in a foul mood because he had to be near the courtroom, if not physically in it, for at least four or five hours each day, trapped by impossible litigants presenting the thoroughly uninteresting testimony of accountants and engineers who were accused of cornering the market on some arcane piece of oil-field equipment the judge did not understand. The parties had rejected his settlement advice, and he was angry about that, especially with a defendant insurance company that had refused to pony up a million or two at his suggestion. There was only so much he could do to punish this defendant, since this was a jury trial, but he was getting in his jabs from the bench every chance he got.

Now here was—guess what—another recalcitrant insurance company creating another mess that was headed for trial in two weeks. The judge ignored those seated before him for a minute, then he raised his eyes.

"What can I do for you today, gentlemen?"

Protocol dictated that the plaintiff talk first, so Tubby began.

"You'll remember this one right away, Judge. My client, Sandy Shandell, went to see Dr. Feingold for cosmetic skin treatments. The treatments were supposed to darken his skin color. This was for cosmetic purposes. There is no medical basis for performing treatments like these, still . . ."

"Your Honor," Guyoz, the insurance company's lawyer, interrupted, "that's absolutely not true. It's experimental, but Sandy Shandell signed all of the necessary disclosure and consent forms."

Judge Maselli held up his hand and stopped Guyoz. "One at a time. Mr. Dubonnet can finish what he has to say. Then you'll have your turn."

"All right, Judge," Tubby resumed. "In any case, the treatments—if that's what they were—were a disaster, and Mr. Shandell is left with these grotesque splotches all over his body. He's an entertainer . . ."

"He's a transvestite stripper," Guyoz interrupted.

Tubby spread his arms and put on a helpless look.

"Let him finish, Mr. Guyoz," the judge snapped.

"Yes, Your Honor," Guyoz said.

"It's true he's a dancer, but he's a popular one. He makes an excellent income. Now, as a result of what the doctor did, he is often too inhibited to perform and needs reconstructive surgery. Even with that he'll never be the same. We calculate his lost income to be in the neighborhood of two hundred fifty thousand dollars and change, his corrective surgery to be at least that much, and for pain, and obviously the tremendous embarrassment he has suffered, three million dollars."

"Now, there's your side." The judge turned his head, making Tubby think of the turret of a tank. "You can have your say now, Mr. Guyoz."

"Thank you, Judge. What we have here is an outrageously inflated claim. Mr. Dubonnet's client is a sex show stripper . . ."

"Dancer," interrupted Tubby.

"Dancer, whatever. He or she, whichever may be correct, works in various French Quarter establishments, where people go in for that kind of thing, and she makes tips or whatever people stick in her garters."

"Wait a second . . ." Tubby began.

"At least that's what she was doing the night I went there."

The judge looked interested.

"Yes, Your Honor, I went to see how her supposed injuries were affecting her performance."

"And?" Judge Maselli raised his eyebrows inquiringly.

"As far as I could tell, those freaks will pay as much to see a splotchy transvestite as one who looks normal."

"Judge . . ." Tubby began, but he was cut off by Maselli's raised palm.

"Mr. Guyoz. We are not going to let this matter, or this trial if we have to have one, degenerate into name-calling, insults, or the use of words like 'freaks.' "

"Sorry, Your Honor."

"Let me finish. Whether you approve of them or not, these clubs give a certain atmosphere to our city that we appreciate. I understand that you may not be aware of this. In Baton Rouge, where you practice law, they may not do things this way. But you do your cause no good when you use expressions like that. I probably shouldn't say this, but you also do your cause no good when you acknowledge to me that the plaintiff has a splotchy appearance and when you distinguish that from a normal appearance. If you are conceding that he, or she, is no longer normal, is this case only about the measure of the plaintiff's damages?"

"Judge, I do practice in Baton Rouge, but I also keep an

office here which I will be frequenting until this trial is concluded. And I am not conceding anything. You should not take my remarks to mean that Shandell has been made any less normal by Dr. Feingold. I'd say she never was normal. What we do know is she wanted to undergo a new and experimental procedure to darken her skin, knowing full well, after being adequately informed, that it had a good chance of failure and that, plain and simple, it didn't work as well as she wanted. She is not ruined, Judge, and these splotches probably make her even more attractive to the customers of these unique joints."

"Mr. Dubonnet, I see you want to talk."

"It's not really about how her customers feel, Judge, it's how she feels. This is a person with feelings like you or me. She is embarrassed and humiliated about the way she looks, and she can't do a thing about it. She wanted to be attractive to her friends and loved ones, and now she's not, or at least so she feels. The disfigurement of her complexion is obvious to anyone, Judge. Maybe she can perform for Mr. Guyoz's 'freaks,' but she wanted more from life than that. She . . ."

"I see what your case will be, Mr. Dubonnet," the judge said. "Okay, let's see where we are. Mr. Guyoz, you heard Mr. Dubonnet suggest that his case is worth more than three million dollars. What do you say to that?"

"I think fifteen thousand dollars is more like it, Judge, and that's just to get rid of it."

"That's a big gap. Eddie, do you have anything to add?"

Eddie Rodrigue had been sitting quietly, bobbing his head in apparent agreement to everything anybody said.

"It seems to me, Judge, that this is a real tough case from all points of view, but I don't think the claims are big enough to touch my client, so like my daddy said I'm gonna 'zip da lip.' "

"Your father was a wise man, Mr. Rodrigue." Judge Maselli closed his eyes for a moment. Then he opened them and said, "It seems to me that both sides here have a problem. You have a problem, Mr. Guyoz, because the disfigurement is apparent. You have a problem, Mr. Dubonnet, because we don't know what value a jury might place on lost love in a case of this sort. Go out in the hall. If you work anything out, let me know. If you don't, be here at eight-thirty Thursday-a-week for jury selection."

"Thank you, Judge," all three said in unison.

The talk in the hall did not amount to much. Guyoz said he still thought Shandell's case stunk, and Tubby said he was going to be surprised how sweet it smelled to a jury.

"We're going to get a jury of the kind of people who understand a guy like Sandy," Tubby told him. "They're going to understand how he's been damaged, and let me tell you, if you don't know it, that you've got another big problem. There is no way that Dr. Feingold can't look rich and conceited. He is rich and conceited, and the man is no actor. The jury will have no pity on him. Plus he knows he botched this up, and he feels sorry for Sandy. That's going to come through to the jury loud and clear."

"So what are we talking about here, Dubonnet? Fifty thousand dollars? Seventy-five thousand?"

"A lot more, Guyoz. Think three hundred thousand as a settlement amount. I believe a jury will give me a lot more."

"I'd send my son to Southern before I'd recommend paying that much to Sandy Shandell."

"That stuff doesn't work in Orleans Parish, man. You

might as well get your checkbook ready. And you're not doing Dr. Feingold any good. The jury is going to hurt you so bad you'll probably cancel his insurance."

"Like I told you before, you want to talk to Feingold and try to work something out, be my guest," Guyoz said. "He's got a twenty-five-thousand-dollar deductible to be concerned about. What I'm concerned about is the Goodhealth Insurance Company, and they're not paying two hundred seventy-five thousand to a male stripper with adjustable boobs. You can tell that to Mr. Shandell, and he can stuff it wherever it feels good."

Guyoz twisted his mustache menacingly. He stuck his briefcase under his arm and marched away.

"That man needs to learn to lighten up," said Eddie.

"He's a prick," Tubby said. Tubby tried to maintain an attitude that any opponent who did not wish to settle with him was a prick, but he thought Guyoz probably really was a prick. And he had hair growing out of his ears. Fuck him.

Tubby made himself a quick salad at a little place near the courthouse that charged you by the ounce. He stared discontentedly at his nutritious plate and thought of finer things. He conjured up sautéed shrimp with roasted peppers and bright little roma tomatoes, and some pasta with a light buttery sauce, like he could be eating at Romairs if the world were just a little less imperfect and there were just a bit more time in the day. Surely, however, there was nothing better for the soul than lettuce, cucumbers, and sweet onions. Feeling pure of heart, Tubby hurried on his way.

Back at the office he scooped his messages from the clip on Cherrylynn's desk. He flipped through a couple. There was one to call Clifford Banks. He went to sit at his desk. Cherrylynn had moved in one of the chairs from the conference room while Tubby's leather chair was at the shop. He drummed his fingers on the armrest while he stared at the message. Then he made the call.

"This is Tubby Dubonnet. Is Mr. Banks in?"

"Just a second, sir, I'll see."

A few moments passed before Banks took the call.

"Hello, Tubby, how are you?"

"I'm peachy, what's the deal?"

"If you would like to meet, let me suggest a spot Uptown."

"All right."

"There is a K&B drugstore not far from your house where Napoleon and Claiborne Avenues intersect." Tubby was sure he had never mentioned where he lived to Banks. There was no big secret, of course, since he was in the phone book.

"Yeah, I know where it is."

"Go there this evening around eleven o'clock. Park away from the store and wait in your car."

"Okay. Who do I look for?"

"Somebody will find you. It will only take a minute."

"You can bet the place I'll be waiting will be well lit."

"As you wish. All they want is the money, Tubby. That's all they ever wanted."

And the son of a bitch hung up.

The phone rang again.

"Hello, Daddy."

"Hi, Debbie, what's going on?"

"I'm going to come downtown in a little bit to see if

Hiller's can fix the gold chain you gave me for Christmas.
I thought maybe you would have time for a cup of coffee."

"Why, sure I would. What time do you think you'll be
here?"

"Maybe three-thirty. Should I come up?"

"Yeah, sure. Come on up and rescue me. We'll go out
and get something to eat or drink, you name it."

"All right, Daddy, see ya."

And the phone rang again.

It was Cherrylynn, reporting that Jynx Margolis wanted
to talk to him. He said he would take the call.

"Hello, Tubby. What the hell is that?"

"What?" Tubby was confused.

"Some kind of damn roach just ran through my kitchen.
Just a minute. Arlene! Arlene, did you see that enormous
roach over there? See if you can't capture that creature and
show him the way home. Tubby, doesn't this city drive you
nuts? My house is clean, but they come in off the streets."

"They must know where the best places are to eat. Take
it as a compliment, Jynx."

"I guess I might as well. Tubby, the reason I called is I
need some money. You can understand that, I know. When
are we going to make that pissant pay me?"

"The hearing is," Tubby checked his calendar, "the six-
teenth. But look, toots, you need to get all your bills
together. You need to be able to lay it all out why three-
thousand-dollars-a-month alimony *pendente lite* isn't enough
to get by on.

"I'd like to see you, or Byron, or Judge whatever-his-
name-is get by on that."

"I didn't say we could, but you need to get your bills together anyway. Byron is paying the mortgage, and I can't promise you that the judge will think you're getting shorted. You'll have to make a case."

"I have plenty of bills, but they're all in a box."

"Well, get them out. You know, your hairdresser bill from Salon Senoj, your manicure bill, the French spa, all those important expenses."

"Tubby, you're fantastic."

"Come see me next week. I'll take you to lunch."

"Okay, dear." She hung up. Tubby started to plan his evening, but the phone rang again.

Debbie suggested La Madeleine in Jackson Square, but Tubby did not want to go so near the scene of last night's violence. There had been nothing about it in the newspapers. He was still shaking, and it would have helped him to see the whole thing objectified in print. Instead, he and Debbie walked to a pastry shop on Gravier Street, where both ordered coffee and almond croissants. Tubby slathered butter on his.

"You don't seem like you're really here today, Daddy."

"Sorry, lots of work. Ignore it."

"Mother said you are paying for Christine's trip to Europe."

"That's right."

"I think it's so neat she's getting to go."

"Me, too. I wish you'd had the chance in high school."

"I'm thinking of going next year after I graduate."

"Let's talk about it when the time gets a little closer. How is summer school going?"

"Okay, I guess. Lots of term papers to write. My problem isn't with school."

"What's your problem with?"

"I probably shouldn't tell you. I'm not sure Mom wants you to know, but it's Harold. He's been staying at my apartment for nearly a month now. I told him he could stay there while he looked for a place to live, which I thought might take him a week or two, but he's moved in nearly everything he owns. I can hardly walk around in there, and I don't know what to do."

You would think if you got divorced you wouldn't have to worry about your ex-wife's deadbeat brother, but no such luck.

"Have you tried asking him to leave?"

"Yes, but he's very good at ignoring me. It's hard to evict your uncle. But I'm going to have to get him out of there, or my landlord is going to kick me out."

"What for?"

"This is the part I'm probably not supposed to tell you. Evidently Harold has been dealing drugs, which I knew nothing about, honestly. He got in a big fight with some guys he brought to my apartment last week while I was at school. The landlord called the police."

"Did they come out?"

"Yes, and they got everybody to quiet down. They didn't arrest anybody or anything, but my landlord is really uptight about it, and really, Daddy, I don't need this going on at my apartment."

"You want me to help you throw him out?"

"I feel so bad saying it, Daddy, but what else am I supposed to do?"

"Look, you tell him he has to move out immediately. If that doesn't work, I'll come over this weekend and put his stuff on the street. You can mention that to him."

"Thanks, Daddy. It's just that it sounds so mean. I don't know where he's going to go."

"Harold is almost thirty. He can figure it out."

"I guess." She was happier now. They finished their coffee, and Tubby walked her back to her car.

Over the throb of "Shake Your Body for Me," Ali heard one of the girls scream in the back. He moved fast, leaving the bar and its sad-eyed customers to fend for themselves. He stepped past the sign marked PRIVATE and pushed open one after another of the doors to the rooms where the girls got dressed and sometimes gave quickies to the men who wanted them. Behind the third door a black girl named Jodi was sprawled on the floor, bleeding from her nose, shaking the cobwebs out of her head.

Standing over her was the short, fat deputy named Freddie.

Freddie swung around menacingly. "Get the fuck out of here," he yelled at Ali.

"I know you, asshole," Ali said to Freddie as he stepped in and swung his big right fist, holding a banana-sized leather-covered blackjack, in a wide arc that ended right between Freddie's eyes. Freddie's legs gave way, and he collapsed with a soft thud on the floor.

"Go somewhere else," Ali told the lady.

He picked up Freddie and slung him over his shoulders. The back door opened onto an alley. In the daytime, when the ice-cream shop next door was open, it was a tourist byway. At night, only things with four feet skittered through. Ali stuck his head outside and saw no one. He ran with the body about twenty yards and dropped it in a pile on the cobblestones. Then he ran back inside his club and bolted the door.

A little later a city policeman on horseback clopped slowly down the street. The horse, more than the officer, found the body, and lowered his nose to investigate. After inspecting the heap from his saddle for a full minute, the policeman dismounted. He rolled Freddie over, compared notes with his horse, and then radioed for backup and an ambulance to the morgue.

For an hour, the alley was full of people and flashing lights, then it was empty and dark again.

"The little fat fuck had an accident," Ali told Monique on the telephone.

SEVENTEEN

Tubby pulled into the parking lot at the K&B drugstore and cruised around to a space some distance away from the store as he had been told. He parked directly under a street lamp. He waited, watching cars come and go. Some kids, who should have been home at that hour, coasted through on bikes. Last-minute shoppers went in and out of the store. On the streetcorner a fat lady with a pink dress, wearing a frayed straw sombrero, was selling hot tamales from a banged-up wagon. Her stand was illuminated by the hot phosphorous glow of a camping lantern. Tubby was checking out an old man pushing a shopping cart up the broken sidewalk, when a tap on the passenger window startled him. His partner, Reggie, opened the door and got in beside him.

"Hello, Tubby," Reggie said softly.

Tubby was almost too surprised to speak, but he managed, "Hello, Reggie. I didn't really expect to see you."

"Yeah, well, that's the way the King Cake crumbles."
He looked in the backseat and saw the gym bag. "Is that
the money?" he asked.

"Most of it. You know we could have done this at the
office, or your house or mine."

"This is the way they wanted it, Tubby. I'm just doing
as I'm instructed."

"What's your interest?"

"That's a little complicated, Tubby."

"Are you just the money handler, Reggie?"

"You could put it that way. Sometimes you get messed
up in things that won't let go of you."

"And that's when you need a lawyer."

"I need a priest, not a lawyer, Tubby. When the DEA
boys show up as planned but the treasure chest is completely
empty, and suspicious people think it's your fault, you need
more than a lawyer. Let's see what's in the bag."

Tubby turned around and got it out of the backseat.

"You sure got me this time," he said to Reggie and
handed over the prize. Reggie settled it on his lap and
unzipped it. He took a quick look inside.

"That's a lot of cash," he said to himself. He didn't dig
around; he just rubbed his chin and looked at Tubby. He
took off his glasses.

"Would you do me a favor?" he asked.

"What's that?"

"Drive up Napoleon Avenue until I tell you to stop. I've
got to turn this over to somebody else."

"I'm not leaving here, Reggie. I've gone as far with this
as I want to go."

"It's not like anything is going to happen to you. I mean,

what worse could happen? I'm sorry about your chair and the painting. Honestly, Tubby, I only just found out a little while ago about your trouble in the French Quarter. I had nothing to do with that. I think they were kind of afraid to send another stranger to see you. They thought maybe you'd go off your rocker."

"So they sent someone I trusted?"

"That's basically it. But they really don't trust me too much, and I've got to take them seriously. I'm scared as shit myself. They told me to get you to drop me off at a particular place on Napoleon, and then you drive away. That's how I'm supposed to take the money to them. I'm the one taking the risk. It's not like I get to make the rules. I'm under a little stress here, too."

"Shit," Tubby said. He started the car.

"Thanks, Tubby," Reggie said. He zipped up the bag and put it between them on the seat. "Just drive up Napoleon toward the Lake."

Tubby rolled out of the lot. A block from the drugstore the wide street turned residential, and a ceiling of live oaks absorbed the streetlights and urban sounds and restored the tropical night. There wasn't much traffic.

"Where to?"

"Right up to the end, by all that construction."

He was talking about an area where two boulevards intersected, and where the city had kept the streets torn up forever for a drainage-improvement project. No one could say when it would be finished.

"Give me a little background here, Reggie. How did you get into this?"

"Just doing what I do best," Reggie sighed. "Putting

Larry, Curly, and Moe together. You know me—slide in, slide out. Only this time I haven't been able to slide out yet."

"It looks like you've got more hands-on involvement than is your usual style, Reggie."

"Yeah, Tubby. I made a mistake there. What I did wrong was I tipped off our esteemed Sheriff to the transaction. He has such a twisted mind, much more so than mine. He immediately liked the idea of ripping off the whole gang of thieves. Several of them were his friends, of course, but they hadn't cut him in, so taking their money appealed to the Sheriff's sense of justice. It was only a game to him, though. He didn't have to put up anything to play. He just donated some dim-bulb muscle men who transformed a profitable investment venture into a murder case."

"What were you going to get out of it, Reggie?"

"Money. Half of what's in this bag. As you know, I love money. Now I'll be lucky to get out of this with my good name and reputation intact. Nobody better find out about my side deal with the Sheriff." He looked soberly at Tubby, who stared straight ahead, driving carefully.

"You were going to screw your clients," Tubby mused.

"That I was."

"Well, you fooled me, Reggie. You turned out to be an asshole after all." Now what is he going to do about me? Tubby wondered.

"Right over there. That's the spot." Reggie directed Tubby into a sort of cul de sac where the road was supposed to go but was now blocked by a steep pile of dirt. Traffic had been routed away onto a long crescent of temporary blacktop around the construction.

Tubby stopped the car and let it idle. It was very dark. "This is far enough for me," Tubby said.

"Take a walk with me," Reggie said. He had put his glasses back on.

Tubby looked at him and shook his head.

"Let's go," Reggie told him. He showed Tubby the gun he was holding in his lap. It was a medium-size .38, and Reggie cocked it.

"Why, Reggie, you surprise me again. I guess this means our partnership is over. You can have my clients."

"Thanks a million, Tubby. A joke a minute, right? I need you to get out of the car with me."

"If you're going to shoot that thing, go ahead. I'm not getting out of the car."

"If you make me shoot you here, which I will, it's going to mess up my plans, and I'm going to have to take it out on one of your darling girls. I'm not saying which one. You want to pick her right now?"

Tubby was looking at a fiercer face than he had ever seen on his partner before. Did Reggie have this much backbone, or was he bluffing? Their eyes held. Tubby blinked first. He turned away and opened the door.

"That's two for you tonight, Reggie. You're showing me talent for chicanery and deception I didn't know you had."

"Thanks, Tub. Just keep on talking."

They both got out of the car. Reggie pointed with his gun into the darkness, in the direction of a path around the sand pile.

"You might as well carry this for me," he said, handing Tubby the gym bag. Tubby started walking where he was told to walk, with Reggie behind him.

The whole area was surrounded with bright-red plastic fencing, and what had formerly been a wide street was now an excavation twenty feet deep and twice that wide. Like many New Orleans boulevards, these streets were built on top of vast concrete tunnels designed to carry off millions of gallons of rainwater. In a typical deluge they would fill up quickly. If it lasted more than thirty minutes or so, the pumping stations that forced the water uphill to Lake Pontchartrain six miles away would reach capacity, the tunnels would back up, manhole covers would pop off and release geysers, and the streets would start to overflow onto lawns and over doorsills. The city's effort to increase pumping capacity and build ever-greater drainage systems was an engineering drama that had been going on for three hundred years. The project on Napoleon Avenue seemed to local residents to have been going on for much of that time.

Tubby and Reggie stepped over the plastic fence and walked along the side of the dark ditch. Around them were cranes, bulldozers, and pile drivers, idle and caked with mud, waiting for the morning. People didn't walk around the neighborhood here at night anymore. Tubby hoped for a watchman. The locals kept their doors and windows shut to try to block out the incessant roar of pumps and generators that labored day and night to move the sludge along. In the daytime this constant noise became background for pile drivers on tall cranes that slammed creosoted timbers, bigger than telephone poles, deep into the muck to support the concrete floor of the new expanded culvert. Construction pipes and steel reinforcement rods were stacked all over what used to be sidewalks.

There was an overgrown kids' playground by the trench,

and Reggie took Tubby there. He sat down as if to rest on
a pile of pipe next to the open chasm of the unfinished canal,
the pistol held loosely in his hand. A cat, almost invisible
in the night, ran across the playground and nuzzled up
against Reggie's leg. He brushed it away with the barrel of
the gun.

"Take your wallet out of your pocket very carefully,
Tubby, and give me whatever money is in there."

"What for?"

"You're being mugged. I'm afraid you're going to be
another victim of urban crime."

Tubby reached into his pants for his wallet and as he did
so asked, "Is this really necessary, Reggie?"

"I'm afraid so. I know you very well, and for a crooked
man you're straight as an arrow. Darryl's dead, and you
won't be able to let me get away with it. All of this would
have been avoided if Darryl had just had the money with
him when he went for the dope, like he was supposed to.
The fact that he didn't is still confusing to me, because if
he planned to rip us off, Champs would have been put out
of business, all legal, in about forty-eight hours. This should
have been a win-win situation for me. I would have done
all right if the deal had been consummated, and even better
if we had snatched the payroll. I didn't make any plans for
ending up with no dope and no dough. Now I've got more
dissatisfied partners than you'd ever believe. And I've got
to break up my happy marriage with you."

"Why didn't you ask Darryl for a refund?"

"Darryl refused to give it back until he saw what we were
going to do to take care of his case. He knew you weren't
in on the transaction, but he was unusually clever when he

gave you the money to hold. He knew it wouldn't occur to us right away that you had it. At least that's what I think Darryl was thinking. He never told me. Then the fool got killed."

Tubby handed over the few bills from his wallet. Reggie took them and said, "Toss your wallet on the ground and hand me the bag, homeboy. You're staying here."

"It's all yours," Tubby said and passed the bag like a basketball right at the gun. He stepped in with it and tried for a field goal at Reggie's crotch. He connected at the same time Reggie fired. The muzzle was in the gym bag so some of the sound was trapped. Tubby felt a pain in his side but it did not stop him from catching Reggie on the chin with his right fist. It was a solid shot, making upward contact while Reggie was bending downward to deal with the pain in his groin, and it caused Reggie to stumble backward over the stack of pipe and into the hole behind him. He didn't even yell. And he had the gym bag with him.

Was that it? Tubby's adrenaline was pumping. He boxed the air, looking for an opponent. Come on, Reggie. Stand up and fight, he was thinking. You're not going down that easy, are you? It's all on the line now, partner. He pivoted, fists up, but nobody was sneaking up behind him. He faced off to the sides. Nothing. So he dropped his hands.

Tubby leaned over the grimy pipes and tried to see down in the ditch. There was a little light from the boarded-up convenience store on the corner, and he thought he could make out something floating around that could be Reggie. There was a rough wooden ladder leaning against the side of the excavation. Tubby was tempted to leave Reggie where he was, but the thought that he might need medical attention bothered Tubby. Also, he hated the idea of leaving all that cash down there for some Boh Brothers employee to find.

He got on the ladder and started down. It was like a cave. After his first step, he remembered that his right side was hurt. He felt the area around his belt, and it smarted, but it did not feel too serious. He went down a little farther. The bottom rungs were in gray soupy water, being sucked gently along by the pumps making the racket overhead. He tentatively put one foot into the water and connected with something solid about calf deep. It all smelled like ripe sewage, but it was cool down here. Tubby splashed along until he reached Reggie's legs, which were sticking up out of the water. The rest of Reggie was submerged. The gym bag bobbed up and down by his feet.

"Looks like one for me," Tubby muttered to Reggie's feet. "You were a hell of a lawyer, but not much of a street fighter."

Tubby picked up the wet bag and sloshed over to the ladder with it. He lodged it against the wall. Then he went back and got Reggie. He floated him over to the ladder and hoisted him onto his shoulders. Good thing he wasn't a heavy guy. "Looks like my ol' partner ain't going to make it," Tubby told himself out loud. Being around death was uncomfortable. Tubby's hands were shaking. But he had been there before. He collected himself.

It took a struggle, but he got the body and the money back up the ladder. He lay beside the quiet form on the grass and panted. Nobody seemed to have taken any notice of anything that had happened. Cars still drove by on the other side of the construction, and the pumps droned on. What could he do with Reggie?

Tubby looked around while he caught his breath. The gray cat came over to investigate, then leaped away when Tubby blew at it. He started to pay attention to a pile driver at the far end of the playground. It was cordoned off by plastic fencing. What he was looking at was its massive cylindrical weight, taller than a man, suspended by cables in the air. He got to his feet and went over to get a closer look. Climbing over the fence, he saw that the weight was positioned over a hole bored in the ground. Tubby couldn't see what was down there, but it must be one of the pilings. The hole was about eighteen inches in diameter. He scraped some gravel down it, but he heard no sounds of the rocks hitting. It looked like the crew had knocked off in the middle of the job.

Tubby went back and got Reggie. He dragged his partner to the fence, rolled him under it, and got him up to the hole. He placed Reggie's legs in the shaft, and then slid the rest of Reggie in. Poor Reggie made no complaint. Tubby pushed some dirt into the hole after him. Then a lot more dirt. Then he crossed himself.

Tubby limped back to his car and drove home, trying to make the sick feeling go away. Wait until later. He left the muddy gym bag in the front hall, put his clothes and his shoes in the washing machine, then walked naked to the shower. He stayed under the hot water for a long time trying to get rid of the smell. When he got out, dawn was just beginning to break. He dressed and got back in the car. He picked up a large coffee at the McDonald's drive-through on Claiborne, then cruised slowly back up Napoleon. Traffic was beginning to move downtown. A paperboy worked steadily up the street pitching the *Times-Picayune* at front doors. Tubby parked two blocks away from the detour.

To others it might have been a lovely morning. The air was clean, like it had just rained, but Tubby didn't notice it. On the other side of the drainage excavation from the playground, along the one-lane roadway through which traffic was temporarily herded, was a bus stop bench. He sat down and opened his coffee. There was a sweet olive tree in bloom somewhere close by. Its floral perfume drifted past in the little gusts of a morning breeze.

Tubby watched a work crew assemble across the job site. They were also drinking coffee and talking to each other. One of the helmeted black guys started gesturing, and the group broke up. A worker wearing blue jeans and a khaki shirt climbed up into the cab of the pile driver. The machine awoke, letting out a loud pop of steam. It popped again. Then the hammer came down, the sound of another day of work beginning. Tubby took a swallow of coffee and swirled it around with his tongue. Each blow was punctuated by a loud explosion of compressed air. Tubby counted twenty blows before he got up and walked back to his car. Rest in peace, Reggie.

He drove back to the K&B drugstore. As soon as he parked, a pickup truck towing Monster Mudbug's Rolling Boiler on a flatbed trailer pulled in beside him, taking up three spaces. The Monster himself leaned out the window.

"I saw your car, Mr. Tubby, and I wanted you to see my flatbed."

"That's great, Adrian. I'm glad to see you're not driving the Boiler on the highway."

"I'm just using the trailer for long trips. I didn't think I should try to drive the Boiler all the way to Lafitte. I got an appearance at a seafood festival today. And you know I can't afford another ticket right now."

"If you're going to be on the road, it's much better to be legal," Tubby said wearily.

"I know, but it's not always practical." Adrian laughed.

"Very philosophical, Adrian."

"Well, see you later, Mr. Tubby. I just wanted you to see that I was taking your advice. And guess what? I got insurance, too."

"Don't kid me, Adrian."

Adrian laughed again and pulled away slowly. Tubby fished a handful of change out of his pocket and went to use the pay phone at the side of the building. He didn't like talking business on his car phone. He punched in Dr. Feingold's home number.

"Jesus, Tubby, you're up early this morning."

"Sorry if I woke you up, Marty, but listen. I got a way to settle your lawsuit."

"Why are you calling me about that at 7:30 in the morning?"

"Because it's a very good way, but I have to do it quickly. It ends up costing you just five thousand dollars, plus you get to take a nine-hundred-thousand-dollar tax loss."

"Tell me more, Santa Claus."

"It's like this. You put up five thousand dollars. Your insurance company puts up maybe fifty thousand, and an anonymous donor puts up nine hundred thousand in your name."

"What's this about an anonymous donor?"

"Let's just say it's someone with an interest in Sandy's welfare."

"Who would be that interested in his welfare?"

"Maybe his mother. What do you say?"

"I need to think this over, Tubby."

"What's to think over? Besides, you have to decide now. This offer won't wait around."

"All I would put up is five thousand dollars?"

"Correct."

"Well, gee, Tubby, what am I missing here? How can I get hurt?"

"I don't see how. Whether you take the tax write-off is up to you. I'm not saying yes or no. It might be better to forget that part. All I'm saying is the anonymous donor is never going to come forward and say it was his money. Five thousand dollars from you, and a yes right now, and this case is over as far as you're concerned."

"Well, if this donor is putting up that much, why do I have to put up the five thousand?"

"That's for screwing up the operation, Marty. You have to pay something for that."

"Hmmm. All right. What do I have to do?"

"Send me a check for five thousand dollars."

"Okay. What else?"

"Nothing. I'll see you later."

"Call me for lunch."

Tubby hung up and fed the box another quarter. "Do you know how I could reach Mr. Guyoz?"

"Who's calling?"

"Tubby Dubonnet."

"Just a second, I'll see if he's free." Jesus, Tubby thought, this guy must always be at the office.

"Morning, Tubby. I've got a meeting. What can I do for you?"

"I spoke to Dr. Feingold, and I think we can work out a deal. The final number isn't certain, but I need two hundred twenty-five thousand dollars from you."

"The case isn't worth that much. I talked to my people, and I've got authority to settle for seventy-five thousand dollars, and that's all I can do."

"Make it one hundred thousand and meet me at CDC in one hour, and we'll read it into the record."

"That's a proposition I might consider. I'd have to make a call."

"Make your call. It's one hundred thousand. Everybody pays their own costs, how about that, but you've got to waive your subrogation rights back against Dr. Feingold. What he pays, he pays, but he doesn't owe you anything for the deductible."

"I've got to get back to you."

"You need to do that right away. This needs to be done this morning, or I can't put it together."

"Don't rush me."

"I'm rushing you. Remember, we'll eat our costs. Right away you're making five or ten thousand dollars."

"I'll call you."

"I'll be at my office in ten minutes, and we need to be at court before ten o'clock."

They both hung up, seeing who could be first.

Cherrylynn was already there, reading the word processor manual and sipping coffee at her desk. Tubby told her good morning and asked her to call Judge Maselli's chambers to alert Mrs. Maselli that the parties to Shandell versus Feingold would be in early to read a settlement into the record.

Guyoz's call came in before Tubby had a chance to pour a cup of coffee from the pot Cherrylynn had made. "Seems we have a deal at one hundred thousand dollars," he said gruffly. "We'll need a complete release of all claims, of course, and it may be thirty days before we can pay."

Tubby silently snapped his fingers. "Thirty days is okay. You need to release your claims against Dr. Feingold for his deductible, and we need to read it into the record this morning."

"What's the hurry? I've got a deposition at ten-thirty."

"The hurry is right now is when I can put the deal together. It has to be now. You'll be long gone by ten-thirty. Just meet me in Maselli's courtroom in half an hour."

"We'll need to read the release into the record."

"Of course."

"Good."

Tubby flipped through the Rolodex for the number and called Sandy Shandell. The phone rang for a long time. There was a pause after it was picked up before Sandy's voice came through. The hello was rough and not too pleasant.

"Good morning, Sandy. This is Tubby."

"Oh hey, Tubby." He was trying to come around. "What's going on?"

"We're going to settle your case. I need you to come to court, like right now."

"Settle my case? Wait a second, Tubby. I'm a little foggy this morning. What time is it?"

"It's almost nine o'clock."

"I just went to bed a little while ago. Is today the trial date?"

"No. We've got a deal. They're ready to pay us off."

"How much money am I getting?"

"How does six hundred thousand sound? Actually you're getting about one million, but I take one-third as my fee."

Sandy wasn't speaking, then he started bubbling. "Oh, I had no idea. That's not for real. Come on. It's a joke, right?"

"It's great, I know, Sandy. It's such a good deal I can't believe it either. But you have to be there, Sandy. You have to run out of your house and catch a cab to the courthouse right now. Am I connecting, Sandy?"

"Yeah, Tubby, sure. I'll catch a taxi. I'll be right there. Tubby, I'm putting on my pants while I'm talking to you."

"Okay, see you." Tubby hung up.

"I'm going to run an errand, then go to the courthouse," he called at Cherrylynn as he rushed out the door. She just waved and kept on typing. The airline ticket office was right around the corner.

Sandy was already pacing in the hall outside the court-room, a morning shadow covering his chin and cheeks, unconcealed by the light powder and rouge he must have applied in the cab. He was wearing patriotic pants, striped red, white, and blue, held up by suspenders with stars on them. He had on a Barcelona Olympics T-shirt commemorating the Lithuanian basketball team. It showed a skeleton making a dunk. He ran at Tubby and gasped in a whisper, "This is so incredible. It's not really happening, right?"

"We'll see. I think it will. Let's go into the courtroom and find out what's going on."

It was motion day, and the courtroom was filling up with lawyers. Up front, Mrs. Maselli was shuffling papers, with a line of attorneys in front of her waiting to sign in. Despite the fact that everyone was wearing a suit, the atmosphere was informal. Lawyers were reading the newspaper, swapping stories, and fixing their makeup. Some were studying their files. A couple of women sat in the jury box, huddled in conversation. Tubby put Sandy on the back row, and tried not to notice that the other occupants of the bench automatically slid a few feet away from him, almost unconsciously. Sandy seemed oblivious.

Guyoz was on the front row writing on a yellow pad braced on his square briefcase. Tubby sat down beside him. They said good morning.

"I've written out the release we'll need," he said.

"I'm sure it's fine." Tubby closed his eyes to rest a minute.

The door to Judge Maselli's chambers opened, and the judge came in fast, in his black robe, and stepped up behind the bench.

"All rise. Oyez, Oyez, the Civil District Court for the Parish of Orleans, State of Louisiana, Division Y, is now in session, the Honorable Dominic Maselli presiding. All quiet in the courtroom," commanded the bailiff.

Papers dropped, conversations stopped, briefcases closed. Tubby jumped up and moved half the distance to the bench, where he stood, politely, waiting for the judge to peer at him over the docket sheet. Finally the eyes came up, and the judge acknowledged Tubby.

"Yes. First we have a settlement to put into the record. Is that right, Mr. Dubonnet?"

"Yes, sir, Judge," Tubby said. He moved to the counsel table, and Guyoz came and stood beside him. Tubby looked to the back and waved up Sandy, who stumbled into the aisle, collected himself, then nimbly pranced to the front to stand behind Tubby.

"Everybody ready?" the judge asked. They nodded. "This is 94-07642. We need the court reporter to take this down."

"Good morning, Judge. I'm Tubby Dubonnet, representing Sandy Shandell, plaintiff, and this is Mr. George Guyoz, representing Dr. Martin Feingold and the Goodhealth Insurance Company. We have a settlement today of this matter, and we wish to read it into the record, Judge, as follows."

Tubby picked up Guyoz's yellow pad and began to read. "The plaintiff agrees to release and forever discharge the defendants from any and all claims he has or may have against either of them arising out of or relating to the medical procedure performed upon him by Dr. Feingold and described in plaintiff's petition, and any and all alleged damages caused to him by the medical procedure. Goodhealth Insurance Company agrees to pay the sum of one hundred thousand dollars within thirty days of this date by check payable jointly to me and to Sandy Shandell. Goodhealth also releases any claims for subrogation or recovery of any deductible in connection with its insurance coverage of Dr. Feingold. Dr. Feingold agrees to pay the sum of nine hundred and five thousand dollars to Mr. Shandell."

Guyoz sat up straight like he had been poked from below, but before he could speak the judge asked, "Is that a total judgment of one million and five thousand dollars, Mr. Dubonnet?"

"Yes, sir."

"Is Dr. Feingold in the courtroom?"

"No, he isn't Your Honor, but his share of the settlement is already paid, and I will state for the record that the judgment is entirely satisfied as to Dr. Feingold at this time."

The judge thought for a second, and then nodded. He asked, "Do you have anything to add, Mr. Guyoz?"

Guyoz could not think of anything, except to say that each party was to pay its own costs. Tubby acknowledged that.

"All right," the judge said. "Is that Mr. Shandell behind you?"

"Yes, it is."

"Do you understand, Mr. Shandell, that you are releasing your claims against the defendants?"

Sandy was in a military mood. "Yes, sir!" he shouted, like a Marine recruit.

"Very well, so entered."

"Thank you, Judge," Guyoz and Tubby said as one.

"What's next?" Judge Maselli asked as they walked out of the courtroom.

Guyoz wanted to talk outside about how Tubby had persuaded Feingold to part with $905,000, but Tubby shrugged him off, and eventually Guyoz stomped off to the elevator. Sandy was rocking up and down on his heels. Tubby was pumped up, too.

"Looks like you struck it rich, Sandy. You want to come by my office after lunch tomorrow, we can cut you a check for six hundred thousand, less whatever I've got in it for costs. When the insurance company check comes in, I'll let you know. You got to be real careful with this money, Sandy."

"I'm going to be real careful, Tubby. I'm going to be ultra-responsible about this. I'm going to put so much aside for living expenses, so much for a sex-change operation, and, of course, I'm going to have a great party. You have to come to that."

"Sure, I'll come. Look, you want to invest some of this money so it doesn't get lost, you come and talk to me. We'll look at some options. This kind of money could cover your bills for the rest of your life if you're smart about it, Sandy."

"I don't know how to thank you, Tubby. I'm buzzing all over. Let's go smoke some pot."

"I really can't right now, Sandy. I've got things to do. But let's get out of here."

EIGHTEEN

TUBBY DROVE TO HIS DAUGH-
ter's apartment building by the 17th Street Canal in Met-
airie. This late in the morning, she would be at school, but
he figured that his ex-brother-in-law Harold would either
be inside sleeping off his evening pizza, or else out by the
pool with the breakfast of champions. Might as well check
the pool first. Good guess—Harold was lying on a lawn
chair with a beer in his hand, a mini-cooler beside him,
doing nothing. A big dog was rolling around in the grass,
but there were no other people around. Tubby thought
Harold might be asleep, but the lad set his beer can on the
concrete when Tubby walked up and put on his sunglasses—
a protective maneuver. Tubby slid one of the plastic pool
chairs over and sat down.

Harold took the initiative. "Hi, Tubby. I didn't know
you were coming. Today's my day off, and I'm drinking a
little beer. Would you like one?"

"No, thanks, Harold. How would you like to get the fuck out of Dodge? You're causing trouble around here. Everybody is getting annoyed."

Harold could deal with that. "It wasn't my fault, Tubby, and I'm really sorry the police came over. I was completely clean, honestly. I know Debbie was upset, and I'm really sorry. As soon as I can get some money together I'm moving. I've got a job starting next week. You know the record shop on Oak Street?"

"Here's a plane ticket to Hawaii," Tubby interrupted, and handed an envelope to Harold. "It's for one o'clock this afternoon. How would you like to go?"

"To Hawaii? I've never been to Hawaii, but I've got some good friends there. Hey, this ticket is for Reggie Turntide."

"I know. He won't be able to use it. It's nonrefundable. They never check the names on the tickets."

"What do you need me to do in Hawaii?"

"Not a damn thing. I just want you gone. I'm paying you to leave. I'll give you five thousand dollars travel money. One thousand right now, and I'll mail you the rest when you get there. Just drop me a postcard and tell me where you are."

"All I have to do is get on the plane?"

"That's right. Clear all your junk out of here. Put it on the street. I don't care where it goes, but it gets out of here. Turn off the AC and leave Debbie's key in the mailbox. Call a cab. The plane leaves in three hours."

"It's a deal, Tubby."

"Pay attention to the fact that that's a one-way ticket, Harold." Tubby gave him $1,000 in cash and left.

* * *

When he walked into his office Cherrylynn reported that Mr. Turntide had not come in, and he had lots of calls. So did Tubby. One of the messages was to call Clifford Banks. Also Mrs. Margolis wanted to come by at one-thirty. He asked Cherrylynn to go down to Mumphries and get him a shrimp po'boy, dressed, and a Barq's red cream soda and whatever she wanted for herself. Tubby pressed Banks's number.

"What happened?" was all Banks said.

"What do you mean, what happened?"

"Where's Reggie?"

"He showed up at the drugstore. He took what I gave him, and we parted company. He didn't come in today. End of story."

"He didn't make an appearance where he was expected."

"That's your tough luck."

"Do you know where I can find him?"

"Reggie and I aren't partners anymore. Find him yourself."

"Goodbye, Tubby."

"Fuck yourself," Tubby thought. Or did he say it out loud?

Cherrylynn came back with the sandwiches. Tubby shut the door to his office and sat at his desk. He really was not hungry. He closed his eyes and thought about the sound of the pile driver. He wondered where the smell of sweet olive was coming from on the forty-third floor.

Clifford Banks took a table in the bar at Champs. He asked the waitress to bring him a scotch and soda and to ask Monique to come over. In a little while she did.

"You wanted to talk to me?"

"Yes, won't you sit down."

"Who are you?"

"My name is Banks. I was associated with Darryl Alvarez in one or two ventures, and I know a little bit about your relationship with him."

Monique sat down. She took a cigarette out of her pants pocket, and he offered to light it. She shook her head and lit it herself from a pack of matches.

"It was very unfortunate what happened to Darryl. I want you to know I had nothing to do with it, and I regret it deeply."

She nodded and exhaled smoke through her nose.

Banks paused to light a cigarette from his own pack.

"Now I am on a quest," he said. "A quest for a million dollars. Do you know where it is?"

She shook her head.

"You see, I was holding it for other investors. People who have done business with me in the past and rely on me not to simply lose their money. They want it back, of course. If I can't find it, I will have to pay it off myself. That is not impossible, but it will certainly have a negative impact on my estate and what I had in mind to leave to my children. Do you understand me?"

"Sure, you're on the hook."

"Well put." He sipped his drink. "I am also looking for a man named Reggie Turntide. Do you know where he is?"

"Never heard of him."

"Medium height, glasses, receding hairline, weak chin?"

That sounded just like the man who drank Wild Turkey,

that first night with Casey, right upstairs. But she shook her head.

"Perhaps we can make a deal," Banks said. "I would be willing to pay a substantial sum, say ten percent, on whatever amount you can help me find."

"I don't know where your money is, Mr. Banks. And I don't really care. I don't have it. I suggest you ask your partners."

"Partners? What do you mean by partners?"

"The cops you had working for you."

Banks looked puzzled.

"There were no cops working with or for me," he said. "This was a deal just between Darryl and me. Reggie assisted, but we had no police associates."

"The guy you just described had them."

"That's hard to believe."

"Believe it."

"I don't suppose you have any proof."

She opened her matchbook and showed him the writing inside: *Casey, 555–3233.*

"Here, it's yours." She flipped it across the table. "Find out where he was when Darryl got busted. That might tell you something. Ask him where your damn money is. Ask him what he was doing the day Darryl got killed."

"Very interesting," Banks said. "You don't happen to know what department he is in, do you?"

"I think he's some kind of bagman for Sheriff Mulé."

"You don't say." Banks stuck the matchbook in his coat. "I think I'll look him up."

"I'd take some friends with you."

"Oh? Well, thank you for that advice. I do have some friends. I'll have them pay a call on Mr. Casey in my place." He stood up.

"Thank you," he said.

"Pay for your drink at the bar," she said.

He blushed, but she watched as he settled up at the register and left.

The buzz of the intercom woke Tubby up.

"Mrs. Margolis is here," Cherrylynn announced.

"Oh, sure. Wait just a second and show her in." Tubby stretched and rubbed his face. He brushed some crumbs off his shirt and shoved his sandwich aside. Cherrylynn opened the door and permitted Jynx to enter.

"Hello, Tubby." She came over to let him kiss her on the cheek. "Goodness, are you frying fish in here?"

"That's my lunch. I forgot to eat it."

"Busy, busy. First things first. Byron surprised me and mailed a check. The peace bond you put him under must have worked. I want to pay you a little of what I owe you."

"That's great, Jynx. I don't have an up-to-date bill, but I expect it's around six thousand dollars."

"Well, I can't pay that now, of course, but here is a check for two hundred fifty dollars just to show you my good faith."

Tubby sighed and took the check.

"Now let me tell you what the jerk has done. He thinks if he gives me a little money I'll back off the property settlement, but I won't."

Tubby shut her out, and tried to think of pleasant things.

It was hard. The conversation stopped. Jynx was looking at him.

"I'm sorry, Jynx. I think I missed the last thing you said. I'm really tired today. Maybe I'm coming down with something. Could we do this another time?"

"What you need is a good back rub."

"A back rub?"

"Yep, that's what you need. They always work for me."

Now here was the pleasant thought he had been looking for.

"Why don't you give me a back rub?" he asked her. That was blunt, but it gave him a little room to back-pedal if she got mad.

She fluttered her eyelids on purpose. "Well, I suppose I could, counselor."

"Let's get out of here."

"Will this come off your fee?" She looked coy.

"I try to return favors," Tubby said, "but I never cut my fees." Like hell.

Monique walked through the door marked DUBONNET & ASSOCIATES. She had made an appointment, and Cherrylynn showed her into Tubby's office.

"Mr. Dubonnet?"

"Yes."

"My name is Monique, from Champs."

"I know who you are. Please sit down." He showed her to one of the upholstered chairs. His tone was soothing, and Monique felt very calm, for a change, like she was in the right place doing the right thing.

Tubby took his place behind the desk. He smiled. "What can I do for you?"

"I guess I need to talk to a lawyer."

"Well, that's what I am. What do you want to talk about?"

"I have about fifty thousand dollars to invest, and I would like you to help with that. Also, I have found what I think is Darryl's will. His friend Jimmy gave it to me. I think he left the club to me. Could you help me with that?"

Tubby folded his hands on his desk. He looked content, as if what she had said gave him great satisfaction.

"I'd be glad to," he said. "Extremely glad to."

"There's another thing. I have this problem in Alabama. I'm on probation. I want to get it taken care of."

"That could be complicated, but, sure, I think I can help you with that."

"Also, I need to get custody of my little girl. She's living with my mama."

"It sounds like you've got a lot to talk about. How about a cup of coffee?"

"That would be fine. Could you give me some idea about how much it will cost?"

Tubby picked up the phone to summon Cherrylynn and coffee. "Don't worry about that, Monique," he said. "This one's already paid for."